A Stolen Future

Georgia Rose

1st Edition Published by Three Shires Publishing

ISBN: 978-1-915665-09-6 (paperback)
ISBN: 978-1-915665-10-2 (hardback)
ISBN: 978-1-915665-08-9 (eBook)

Edited by Mark Barry
www.greenwizardpublishing.blogspot.co.uk

Proofread by Julia Gibbs
juliaproofreader@gmail.com

Cover and map design by Simon Emery
siemery2012@gmail.com

British Library Cataloguing in Publication Data
A CIP catalogue record for this book is available from the British Library

OTHER BOOKS BY GEORGIA ROSE

The Grayson Trilogy

A Single Step (Book 1 of The Grayson Trilogy)

Before the Dawn (Book 2 of The Grayson Trilogy)

Thicker than Water (Book 3 of The Grayson Trilogy)

The Joker (A Grayson Trilogy Short Story)

The Ross Duology

Parallel Lies

Loving Vengeance

A Shade Darker

A Killer Strikes

Shape of Revenge

Hard to Forgive

Table of Contents

Author's Note

1: A Chip off the Old Block? 1

2: Not His Father Then 14

3: Intuitive? 23

4: Clean-Ups and Break-Ins 35

5: Whistle-blower 42

6: Spectator Gold 52

7: The Welcome Return of Coffee and Cake 61

8: An Unexpected Visit 69

9: A Time for Action... and Reaction 79

10: The Six Ps 101

11: Ham and Pineapple 105

12: My Trail of Breadcrumbs... 121

13: The Unexpected Turn of Events 142

14: A Warring Couple 158

15: Downfall of the King 165

16: A Mother Scorned... 182

17: Topsoil 186

Epilogue 210

Get Free Exclusive Content by Signing up to the Georgia Rose Newsletter

Acknowledgements

Contact details

A Map of this part of Melton and Buntingley

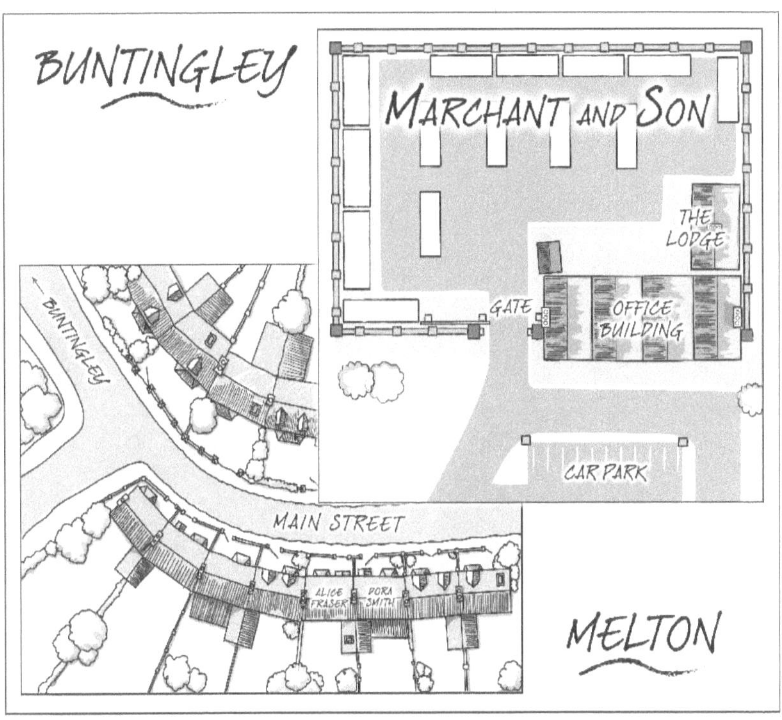

It is said it takes a village to publish a book, and as I struggled with this one, those words have never been truer.
This book is therefore dedicated to all those in the acknowledgements who helped me out of the dark places I found myself in while trying to pull this novel together.

Author's Note

Please note that while *A Stolen Future* is a standalone story it is the fourth book in the *A Shade Darker* series and I have written these books to be read as a series. I do not rehash what happened in the first three books, *A Killer Strikes*, *Shape of Revenge* and *Hard to Forgive*, or provide long explanations. From the beginning of this novel, there are spoilers that will affect your enjoyment of the previous books. Once seen, those things can never be unseen. So, if you haven't read *A Killer Strikes* already you can find it wherever you buy your books. Reading the earlier books in the series also means you won't miss out on meeting the fabulous characters who live and work in the village of Melton.

Thank you

Georgia

"Some people will label you as vindictive, unforgiving or even evil for not allowing them to hurt you, yet again."
Wayne Gerard Trotman

1: A Chip off the Old Block?

There had been a moment, once, a long time ago now, when Mr Marchant Senior had casually placed his hand on my bottom. I had only brought the post into his office to be signed and was therefore far too surprised to react. Unexpected. That's what it was. Badly timed too. What with him being married. Happily, by all accounts, although since that incident I wasn't so sure. I'd even speculated that maybe, just maybe, something was missing from his world, despite the carefully crafted façade of family man, local philanthropist, head of a building empire.

That touch had held such promise, although it lingered but a moment. And it was thrilling. All these years later, I could still recall the sensation, the tingle.

Sadly, it was all I had left of what might have been. Because now, my world was a different place, and I didn't care for it.

I hear Rex call me, not by name, of course. An abrupt, 'Come here,' is barked out instead. I used to ignore it, pretend he was calling someone else. A passing dog, perhaps. But that only made matters worse.

I pick up my pad and pen and hurry to his office, reflecting on the fact Mr Marchant Senior had always had the grace to call my extension if he wanted me to come through. Not that he'd often needed to. In those days, both his and my office walls were glass and he could easily get my attention without the need to shout.

I enter Rex's inner sanctum.

'Where's my dry cleaning? My suit? I need it tonight.' Hands behind his head, he leans back on his executive chair behind the expansive desk on which there is precious little sign of any work being done.

'You haven't asked me to collect any dry cleaning.' My voice breaks as I speak and I clear my throat, my mouth dry as I stare down at my pad, at recent instructions. No. No mention of dry cleaning. He leans forward. His close-set eyes are eager, like those of a bird of prey, its target in sight.

'Yes, I did. You said you'd pick it up and bring it in this morning.'

'Did I?' The furrow deepens between my eyes as I struggle to remember.

'Clearly you've forgotten, so go get it now.'

'I'm in the middle of—'

'Now.' He slides a single sheet of paper, which he pretends to read, across the polished mahogany and I know I'm dismissed. I stifle my sigh of frustration as I return to my office to retrieve my handbag and keys. It's a pain when interruptions break the flow of me putting the monthly finance reports together. I like to follow my tried and tested process so nothing gets missed. Plus, it's also my lunch hour. It isn't a long journey back to Sharon's Stores in Melton, a round trip of ten miles, but as I live in Melton, it would have been far easier if I could have run the errand on the way to, or from, work. Also, this interruption means I'm unlikely to get the reports completed this afternoon and Rex does like them done on the first of the month. Why, I haven't yet fathomed, as I'm sure he never so much as glances at them.

They've not made for pretty reading in months, and yet he's not said a word.

I visit the facilities, thinking it is ironic he wants me to pick up his suit on company time when he never wears one in the office. Jeans and a tee shirt are his usual attire. Although only his. Everyone else wears office clothes, which I prefer anyway. You know where you are with what amounts to a uniform.

Although I will never forget the rather pointed comments he once made, embarrassingly in front of the other staff, joking (and I use that word loosely) about which decade my suits had come from, thus shaming me into replacing my entire workwear wardrobe. An expense I could have done without. Much as I hate to admit it when I'd evaluated my appearance after Rex's rather cruel observations, I had seen how old-fashioned I'd become. How frumpy.

Of course, Mr Marchant Senior had never worn anything less formal than a suit to the office, sometimes a three-piece. I liked those particularly, as I found a well-fitted waistcoat becoming on a man.

I don't even like calling him Rex. His father had been Mr Marchant to me, despite our close working relationship, and I remember clearly the exchange with Rex on his first day. He'd scoffed at me calling him Mr Marchant, which I did out of respect.

'I'm not my father,' he'd spat out through gritted teeth.

No, you're not. But in those early days of the new reign, I'd still had hope the business of Marchant & Son would carry on as before, as would my job. Disillusion followed shortly thereafter.

Before I leave my office, I carefully check through all the recent notes on my pad again. I've taken to writing everything down because clearly my memory is not what it once was and Rex often pulls me up on things I've forgotten. I've also made two serious mistakes in recent months, which had shaken my confidence.

No, there is no mention of any dry cleaning. Not recently anyway. Obviously, I've picked it up before, though why I have no idea as it isn't part of my job description. But then many things I do for Rex I was never called upon to do for his father. I thought it was because of Mr Marchant Senior coming from a different generation. He was more aware of, and sensitive to, *most* of the boundaries of the employer/employee relationship.

I walk out to my beloved car, an original Mini Cooper, surprised it passed the MOT again last month and is therefore good for another year on the road. I'd been concerned it would fail and had lain awake at night fretting over the possibility of having to spend my savings on replacing it. At least that worry is deferred for another year. In dire need of a wash, it is the shabbiest vehicle in the car park. Which is probably the reason Rex withdrew my entitlement to the reserved spot, next to his BMW, that I had with Mr Marchant Senior for so many years. I appreciate from his point of view it isn't the image of success the company wants to project.

I wait as two company vans turn in. One of the site managers, Eddie Lumbers, is in the first, and he raises his hand to me in greeting as they pass by and follow the road round to the rear of the building I work in. There is a huge yard out back which houses the construction machines, vehicles and materials. Running along the far side and forming an L shape with the office block is a large building, called The Lodge, for use by the builders themselves and all the support staff and professionals brought in on projects such as architects and surveyors.

This is the area Mr Marchant Senior loved to spend his time in most and whenever he had the chance, he was at his happiest when he got to change from his office into his work clothes and discuss projects with his men. He took every opportunity he could to visit and spend time on each site for the same reason. Under the new regime, I worry this crucial part of the business lacks guidance and direction.

Despite the excellent project and site managers we have on the payroll, it still needs an experienced someone with a guiding hand in overall control, and that's where there is a problem with Rex. He lacks any credibility, as he hasn't a clue what he is talking about.

I can't help worry, but why I do, I'm not sure. After all, it isn't my company. Why should it bother me if Rex is already damaging its reputation? The reality is I've been part of the business for so long it's difficult not to care and I can't turn my back on something Mr Marchant Senior put so much work into building.

As I leave Buntingley and drive towards Melton, I put Rex out of my mind, as my thoughts wander back to that bottom touch from what I realise is now some eight years ago. I know I shouldn't dwell on it. It's pathetic to do so, particularly after so long, but I have never been able to help myself. What if I'd responded? Favourably, of course. Where might I be now? Not where I am, living in a small cottage and scratching out a living with little besides a state pension to see me through my twilight years, of that I'm certain.

I'd given myself a good talking-to at the time, of course. Told myself George wouldn't have minded. My husband had died far too young, and well before there had been any planning for our old age. Now, although only about to turn fifty, I feel I'm racing towards retirement, and with no one else to rely on for support I've only ever managed to get by and not been in a position to put much away over the years.

'Needs must, old girl,' is what George would have said had I encouraged Mr Marchant Senior. Which is weird now because I was barely twenty when George died. Still, it's what he called me, had done since we'd met in our early teens way back in the 1980s. At the time I'd imagined us growing old together, his endearment becoming more appropriate as the years passed. But that life was all so long ago, and so different from the one I live now. Some days it is as if it hadn't happened at all.

I think they'd have got on, my George and Mr Marchant Senior. They were of the same cut, had the same altruistic nature. I believe it's why I was so drawn to Mr Marchant Senior. He reminded me of my lost love.

I've also recently pondered that one short-lived husband and a bottom touch doesn't amount to much by way of romance in a lifetime. For years after losing George, I hadn't been able to even contemplate getting involved with anyone else. Then I sunk all my energy into working with Mr Marchant Senior to build Marchant and Son into the company it is today. Also, it isn't as if anyone has shown any interest in me in years either, so I'm not exactly inspired to give romance another go. No, when it comes down to it, given the passion, excitement and unpredictability of my early years with George, I've been perfectly happy with my steady job and quiet home life.

I pass the end of Marchant Road, renamed years ago and the clearest indication, if any is needed, of the high esteem Mr Marchant Senior was held in around here. Pulling up in front of the village shop, Sharon's Stores, I get out, wishing I'd had the foresight to put on my coat. Despite it being April, if only the first, there is a chill wind, and I pull my jacket around me as I scuttle across to the entrance. Rain is in the air and spring feels far away.

Sharon sits behind the counter, as usual. She is far too pale, her face drawn and sickly beneath the peroxide hair. I've heard rumours she is ill and undergoing tests but as far as anyone knows there has been no diagnosis as yet. I go straight to the counter and, as I find her prickly to get into conversation with, restrict myself to asking for Rex's suit. Not that it prevents her from prying.

'Do you have the receipt? Oh, and have you heard about poor Dora Smith?' Sharon's hair is like straw, dry and fragile, the ends splitting. I'm relieved I never embarked along the hair-dyeing route. There are some greys on my head, but I have every intention of letting them develop at a pace to lead me elegantly into old age. I smooth my shoulder-length hair with my free hand, to reassure myself it is well-conditioned, then tuck one side behind my ear as I reply.

'No, sorry. Rex has misplaced it.' It's always the same if I'm collecting something for him. I never have the ticket, and I've given up asking him for paperwork. It's as though he doesn't think he need concern himself with such trifling details. He's the same with any receipt or invoice. "Only plebs keep those", he'd once told me when I'd tried to explain their need for my bookkeeping. I ignore Sharon's eye roll as I deflect her second question. 'Dora's a good friend, as well as a neighbour.' *And no, Sharon, I'm not going to gossip about her.*

'There's something funny been going on with her. You mark my words. Mind, you'll know all about it, of course, seeing as how you're *such* good friends.' Sharon makes this nasty dig, I know her too well to take any notice, then tuts as she slides herself off the stool. Rex's name will be on the bag anyway, but I get the impression Sharon likes her customers to be fully aware of just how much they are putting her out. As it is, she goes through to the back and returns mere seconds later with the suit bag. Astonishingly, it hasn't entailed a long hunt after all, as I suspected. Weirdly she strokes her hand down the cover and smiles. 'I bet he looks super in this. He's such a charming young man and so handsome.' My responding smile is stiff but I keep my mouth shut, take out the company credit card, pay, and leave the shop before she can expand on her thoughts about Rex or mention the subject of Dora Smith again.

The rain is insistent now and coming in on a slant, which causes me to duck and tilt my head away from its icy sting as I hustle across the road. Having only two doors on the car, I battle to get the suit bag into the back and hung on the hook. Once I'm in the driving seat, I sweep my wet hair off my face, then remove my speckled glasses and wipe them on the edge of my skirt before turning on the fan as I start the engine to de-mist the windows. It isn't efficient, so as usual I clear the windscreen with a tissue from my bag. Reluctantly, I ignore the call of home and head back to the office, consoling myself by eating the sandwich I'd made for lunch on the way.

My thoughts drift back to Dora. I'm still reeling from her complete breakdown at the weekend. At everything it revealed.

I know it will have shocked everyone who witnessed it, but it had left me with the feeling I'd let her down badly. I believed I knew her and yet I knew nothing.

I check in with Trish Taylor, our receptionist, as I walk back into the office, then I have a quick word or two with the other staff who are at their desks, working my way across the open-plan section until I reach my and Rex's offices at the end. Everything is running smoothly. I deliver the suit to Rex's office and, in his absence, hang it on the back of the door. Then I carry on with the reports, struggling with the new accounting system.

Rex walks in through the main door at nearly four o'clock, after what has clearly been a lengthy lunch. I try to ignore it when he lingers in reception, flirting with Trish and distracting her and me from our work, but it is hard to do given the glass walls and open-plan arrangement.

The way Rex chases after the young women in the company is problematic. Recruitment to replace those who leave fills considerably more hours of my day than it has ever done before. It is only a matter of time before someone sues us.

It's another half an hour before he passes my office and I call out to tell him I'd put the suit on the back of his door, a fact he barely acknowledges. His rudeness, although I should be used to it by now, rankles, so even though I know I shouldn't, I blurt out, 'Also, could you not distract Trish? She has a lot to get through today.' He pauses, retraces his steps, and stands fully in my doorway, his rugby player build intimidating.

'As I'm the one who pays her, I'll decide how she spends her fucking time.' He then walks away to his office. Despite being used to the way he speaks to me, and his language, my heart flutters like a startled moth, and a flush creeps up my neck as I glance over at the cubicles. A couple of curious faces quickly turn back to their screens. I can't condemn their interest because he never lowers his voice, especially if I am the one at the end of some rebuke.

I've spent many years building my position in the company, but now Rex is in charge, any control I had is slipping away from beneath me like scree down a mountainside with me left scrabbling for purchase as he undermines me whenever he has the chance. It isn't on, but no approach to address the matter of the friction between us working together has been successful to date. He cannot take feedback and, as I hate confrontation, I've learnt to back away from giving it. Today is no different and rather than challenge him, which a stronger person would have done. I quietly seethe at my desk instead as I continue to work on my reports.

With my trip out earlier, there is no way I'm going to complete them today so, as five-thirty approaches, I decide I'll finish them the next morning. As I pack away, Rex comes out of his office and into mine with his hand held out.

'Where are the reports?'

'Because I had to get your suit. I wasn't able to complete them, so I'll finish them tomorrow.'

'That's unacceptable. I want them on the first of the month. You know that and I don't want to hear your excuses. You shouldn't have wasted your time going out when you did, should you?'

'But you told me to do it straight away.'

'No, I didn't. Don't twist your failings back onto me. What do I tell you to do?' Then clearly not expecting an answer, he continues, 'Prioritise. I want those reports on my desk first thing, so I suggest you stay and complete them tonight, or maybe you'd prefer to come in early?' He raises his hand, points his finger towards me. 'First thing. No excuses.'

His orders having to take precedence over anything else I might have to do is one thing. But I dislike the fact it then gives him the excuse to complain when I am behind with my own tasks. Consequently I have become resentful, which isn't an emotion I've experienced at any other time in my working life.

I sit back at my desk unable to answer or even look at him any further, so humiliated do I feel. The shame of being spoken to like that by someone young enough to be my son is mortifying and it is all I can do not to cry as I carry on. It isn't like I'm not used to working late but I hadn't planned on doing so today. In reality, it takes me a little over an hour, and once done, I print off the hard copies he asks for. When I go to put them on his desk, the suit is still hanging on the back of the door. I stop and stare at it, then curse under my breath.

The chill wind whips round the corner as I step out of the building later, hitting me with a refreshing blast that's welcome after so many hours staring at a screen. I spot Eddie Lumbers wiping my car down with a chamois, which is a surprise. It looks as sparkly as an old car can manage.

'Thank you, that's kind of you,' I say as I get nearer, delighted as it saves me a job I rarely get round to.

'You're welcome. After being on site I had to wash my truck anyway,' and he gesticulates to his pickup nearby, 'so it was as easy to do yours at the same time.' I smile at him, his face creasing in response, eyes shining. He has a pencil behind his ear as usual. It's replaced "his next cigarette" that he always had lined up there until he quit a few years ago. Even this early in the year, he has a healthy glow about him. I suppose it's from being outside. The silver of his hair, the change that causes the colour to drain from so many people's faces, has no such success in his case. 'You're late finishing.'

'Yes, I had to complete some reports Rex wanted, so it was easier to stay late than to come in early.'

'How conscientious of you.' He grins as I roll my eyes. Eddie and I have never exchanged a word about our lives working under Rex. We don't need to. We both understand the score. Although I've noticed Rex behaves better with those at The Lodge than with those in the office. Eddie hesitates, as though not sure if or how to continue. 'Erm… Do you know how Dora is? I've been worried.' Eddie had been part of the cast for the Murder Mystery evening, so had been witness to the events of last Saturday night.

'It's kind of you to ask after her. I've seen her, and she's feeling better. I think she'll be home early next week.'

'That's good to hear. When you see her next, give her my best, won't you?'

'Of course I will.' We say our goodbyes as I get into my car, relieved to be on my way home at last.

I'd visited Dora at the hospital, with some trepidation, the day after the Murder Mystery. She'd always appeared to me to be one of the strongest women I knew, and I'd worried myself through a restless night as to the damage the ordeal might have caused her. Despite preparing myself, she'd still appeared small in the bed, and fragile, like an injured bird, broken and lost. Beyond the bandages and bruises she'd been calm, although distant, and struggled to concentrate on anything for any period. She'd lapsed into silence mid-sentence and gazed out of the window distractedly. She hadn't wanted to talk for long, had said she was tired and had said nothing about the incident, which I'd understood. Afterwards, as I'd returned to my car, I'd been glad I'd gone, so she'd know I was there for her. I'd also gleaned she was likely to be in hospital until after the coming weekend so, as one practical thing I can do, I am going to carry out a thorough clean of her cottage so it is all ready for her return.

It is harder for me to switch off from work these days. My latest mistake or admonishment from Rex spins through my brain like clothes in a washing machine, often into the early hours. Later that evening, I sit in the quiet with a glass of wine and, as I've done many times before, focus on my work situation. This is the first day in April. Another month having passed by in which nothing has changed. Just like nothing has changed over the last eight years. I've given it enough time to improve, yet it hasn't and now something has to give, because I can't continue to work in that environment.

Despite examining the problem from every direction over the past weeks and months, I can only see one way to resolve the situation and I can't keep procrastinating.

Either I have to go, or Rex does.

2: Not His Father Then

The following morning, my frustration grows further as Rex doesn't appear in the office until eleven.

As his car glides into the car park, the pulse of adrenaline his arrival sparks through my veins is yet another sign of the negative effect his presence has on me.

His lack of work ethic has come as a shock. He rolls into work when it suits. Mid-morning, sometimes not until after lunch, and doesn't even bother making excuses for his tardiness. Why should he? It is his right, after all. He's made that clear.

If he ever arrives on time, then he leaves early. I assume to pursue his playboy lifestyle. Because I can see where he goes and what he does. All of it going on the credit card and, he tells me, all of it tax deductible when I can see it isn't. After all, since when have outings to casinos or strip clubs been business expenses?

When I go into his office to see if he has any special requests for the day, I say, 'You didn't need your suit urgently after all then. That would have saved me a trip.'

'I'll repeat myself as, once again, you've clearly forgotten something I already told you. I never said it was urgent so there was no need to rush out on company time.' He doesn't so much as glance up from his phone as he speaks to me.

Bristling from the unfairness, I counter with, 'It wasn't company time, it w—' only to be interrupted by his raised hand. This is something he does when he's heard enough and I've learned from experience not to carry on talking.

Chastened but fuming, I disappear back to my office, hoping my work will keep me in there and out of his way for the morning. I'm relieved I get to escape today, as it is Thursday. We have a large housing estate under construction in a village on the other side of Melton and on Thursdays I spend the afternoon in the sales office sorting out paperwork and the myriad other issues that crop up with any site.

As my thoughts wander from what I should be doing, I look over at Fiona Stewart working away at her desk, and, for a few moments I study her. She is my extremely competent assistant and deals with a lot of the background accounts work for the business. I am certain that, unlike me, Fiona wouldn't be sent scuttling back to her desk by Rex's slights. She'd stand her ground and have exactly the right words with which to respond.

Of course, women wouldn't put up with bottom-touching nowadays either. Not women like Fiona. Young women. Strong, confident women. She is only twenty-eight, but appears considerably more together than me. At the time of the bottom incident, it hadn't occurred to me to mind. But now? I've seen the papers. The accusations. The men hauled into the glare of public scrutiny. Accused and called to account. I've felt conflicted when reading the stories, because that wasn't him, and it wasn't me. I wasn't a victim. And that wasn't our relationship. I'd never felt taken advantage of. Or considered the moment to be an abuse of position. More a gentle act of affection which sadly, for me anyway, never went further.

Fiona would scoff at me if I told her about it. Not that I would. We don't have that sort of relationship. Anyway, she'd never understand. Different generations.

The truth is it wouldn't have been any great hardship for me to have taken things further. I already loved the man, after all. I had done ever since he took me on. So relieved was I and so grateful for the job. What was there not to love? No tricky questions asked, precious little by way of interview undertaken.

I'd given myself a good talking-to at the time. Told myself if it should happen again I would be brave, maybe place my hand against his, let him know it was all right, he could take it further.

I suppose it is a waste of time to dwell on the matter after all these years, but I do so with a sad fondness because before it could ever happen again, Mr Marchant Senior died, and everything changed.

Of course, I only call him Mr Marchant Senior because there is a younger version too, now. Mr Marchant Senior was not, in fact, much older than me and at the time of the bottom-touching incident I was early forties, he soon to turn fifty. Sadly, he didn't make it that far, dying with his first heart attack while playing golf. No doctor was on the course. No help came quickly enough.

Charlie, his name was to his friends. Charlie Marchant.

I, who fell into a black pit of loss, was certain I grieved more than his widow. Abigail Marchant (who called him Charles) arrived in the office the following day, bright, breezy, and apparently keen to see what was what to ensure their son, Mr Marchant Junior, could take up his position as head of the company, just as soon as he left university. Where, as far as I could tell, he'd spent a considerable amount of time partying hard with his father's money whilst remaining reluctant to attend to any of his studies. I was prepared to be proven wrong, naturally, and as the time approached, I was sure there'd be plenty of celebrating of his degree results. However, instead of rapturous applause and hoorays all round, there was not a flicker of recognition, not a glass raised. The entire three-year debacle was swept under the convenient carpet of duty, of having so much to do, to learn, to take on, which meant leaving the whole messy business of failure behind with never so much as a backward glance.

Maybe Rex's plan all along had been to become involved with Marchant & Son once he had completed his studies, and maybe I'd misjudged him. But despite having worked for his father for so long, I knew little of Rex. Unlike other family firms I am aware of, he didn't hang around the offices or building supplies yard as a child. He rarely visited, in fact. When he did, he'd spend his time glued to a screen slouched in a chair in his father's office and showed zero enthusiasm for the business. Him finding the office side boring was understandable, but he wasn't even interested in the construction vehicles, unlike most young boys.

From what I'd observed I secretly believed Abigail, the widow, felt the building trade beneath her and while she was quite happy to be kept in significant comfort on the proceeds, she didn't want to be involved. Neither did she originally want it for her son, mummy's boy that he appeared to be, no doubt having far loftier ambitions for him than building houses. But, according to local gossip, Rex had shown no eagerness for any other way to earn his living either, so when Mr Marchant Senior died so abruptly, and perhaps conveniently, I could see this U-turn by his mother was her opportunity to keep the money coming in and the company in the family after all. The fact Rex had no experience, little interest and even less aptitude for the business appeared irrelevant to her.

Then there was the hostility.

Over the years, I had tried with Abigail. I had. But it was tough going. And she was the one who made it so, because while I went out of my way to be friendly, courteous and welcoming whenever she came into the office, she was little more than civil, and only that if her husband was within earshot.

I spent a considerable amount of time researching appropriate gifts for her, and Rex, to ensure Mr Marchant Senior looked good. Booking treats and trips for them to enjoy as a couple and as a family was part of my role in the company. I didn't expect thanks because, naturally, everything appeared as though it was from her husband. Out of loyalty, Mr Marchant Senior never said a word, but I could read between the lines of the things he didn't say. Her ingratitude was an indirect insult.

After he died, it changed. Abigail's attitude towards me. Any civility ended; and she was openly hostile.

I would never forget that first morning when she arrived with her beloved son. Wearing an acid green suit and matching stilettos, she told me to follow her into her husband's office, then took the chair behind his desk. I, barely holding myself together, suggested as a mark of respect that perhaps the company should close for the day.

'Nonsense,' she'd said. 'If you lot have so little to do, you can afford to take the time off, then I have a list of jobs at home that will keep you busy.' She was hard to read. Always had been, her face so full of Botox I doubted she'd physically expressed an emotion in the last twenty years. But there was no mistaking the intent behind her next words, the glitter of malice as she made eye contact unmistakable. 'Do not assume any position here, Alice. Do not seek to take advantage or improve your situation in my son's company. You are an employee. That is all. You know how everything works, and that is the only reason we will continue to tolerate you as an employee. If you do not do your job to the level I have been assured you are capable of, then there is no further need for you to remain here. Am I understood?'

Whether she could legally fire me was irrelevant at that moment. I left the room shaken and went straight to the toilets to vomit. The despair that overwhelmed me in the cubicle clung to me for months, deepening my grief and turning my world dark for longer than I cared to remember.

I'd never forgive her for not allowing anyone from the company to attend the funeral, either.

'Family only,' she'd announced, and Mr Marchant Senior's send-off was without the turnout he'd deserved.

I'd had to deal with all the paperwork needed to transfer everything over to Rex. And each piece of the business I unravelled and transferred into the new name, the deeds, the shareholding, the bank mandates, took Mr Marchant Senior that bit further away from me.

I had known from the moment I received the dreadful news of my boss' death that my life had changed once more and I genuinely feared for my future given the threat made so starkly by Abigail. At the same time my loss was hard to bear, but I could hardly make it public. For what would people think? So, while everyone else moved on, I remained unable to accept he'd gone. It seemed impossible to me that someone so vigorous, so full of life could be here one minute and not the next. He had no health issues other than having diabetes since he was a child, and he'd always managed that well. He kept fit and was diligent in taking care of himself. I couldn't get my head round it at all.

The pressure to maintain the impression I was coping was immense and as I struggled on in the first weeks and months to keep things going, I searched for other work. While I did at least have something to put on my CV this time around, the only positions available were little more than minimum wage, and another way Mr Marchant Senior had cared for and appreciated me was to pay me better than I would be likely to receive in the same position elsewhere. It wasn't a huge amount, but being single, I needed that money, if I was going to keep my cottage and what amounted to my otherwise modest existence. Leaving for something that paid worse was going to be difficult. Besides, once I'd got over my initial shock, I felt I owed it to Mr Marchant Senior to stay and help keep the business going. After all, I was no longer just his secretary. Over the years I'd taken on more and more responsibility until I was second-in-command, answering only to the boss himself, with assistants of my own to help with various tasks, and was proud of how I'd built myself up from nothing.

Now, given some distance, I'd perhaps been naïve in taking on so many duties without being rewarded as much as I was probably due. But I'd never felt used or taken advantage of, at the time. Instead, I'd seen the company's growth as something to strive for. The crushing grief that consumed me after Mr Marchant Senior died though, brought home the fact that maybe I'd invested more of myself into the place than I should have done. Despite his assurances he would leave me some shares in the business, he hadn't, and there was going to be no pot of gold at the end of the rainbow for me. Not now Rex was in charge.

Or rather, not now his mother was in charge. I knew who was pulling the strings because I had difficulty believing someone so young could be so bitter. Or nasty.

Rex went back on other promises his father had made to me. A substantial pay rise had been due, together with a bonus for handling a particularly tricky contract. But Rex had come in at precisely the wrong moment and cancelled both.

His exact words were, 'Your existing pay level is way more than you're worth anyway and there's no need for a bonus. You were only doing your job.'

I should have walked out right then, but didn't. My loyalty to his father, my sense of responsibility to keep the business going, kept me in place and conscientious in my work. I gritted my teeth and got on with it.

It wasn't easy.

Despite my experience, and his lack of it, Rex has loosened enough of the foundation beneath my confidence to make me feel as though I don't know what I am doing. Yet he is only too willing to heap the work on me each day while he, supposedly, goes out seeking new clients. Networking is what he calls it. Wining and dining, my preferred term. I know, I see the output of his efforts. The spend on the credit card. The gifts. The extravagance. Something his father had never needed to do. New contracts had flowed his way through honest hard work, through producing an excellent product and having an even better reputation.

While there was plenty of work available in the early days of Rex's reign, it was all courtesy of his father's standing in the area. It is noticeable how the number of new opportunities has dropped off in the last year or so. Now it is purely down to Rex's efforts. The decline is already showing in the accounts. Even Fiona has noticed. It won't be long before this will have a significant impact on the business and, if things don't improve soon, we will face redundancies because we can't afford to pay builders who are idle. But Rex refuses to listen to my warnings and takes no personal responsibility whatsoever for the reduction in work. This is where my concern lies. The future of the company. If it carries on the way it is going, it won't survive, which means a lot of jobs are on the line and I can't help but feel a certain responsibility to do all I can to protect those.

That evening, Rex calls me (which is not okay) to let me know his mother is coming into the office in the morning. Why he rings to let me know or why she is coming in, I'm not sure. He doesn't always tell me, and he never elaborates. But if his intention is to cause me a sleepless night, which I suspect it is, then he is successful.

3: Intuitive?

They arrive in force at an early, for them, ten o'clock. Clearly, Mummy has woken her baby earlier than usual. They travelled in two cars, which is promising, as it means she probably won't be here for long.

Although it will feel long enough.

For no rhyme or reason, Abigail Marchant has taken it upon herself to descend on the office sporadically to do what she calls her "spot checks". This means her asking random questions about the running of everything and anything. I'm not sure why she feels the need to do this, as she has no official place in the business. She has chosen not to be a director as in her words, "that is a man's place". Please… More like she doesn't want to take on any of the responsibility and yet she still considers it her right to keep an eye on things. Or perhaps she just likes to be nosy. She comes in whenever the fancy takes her and, I assume, when she doesn't have anything more pressing on her time; her numerous social engagements, tennis and golf meet-ups, beauty treatments, holidays and so on.

My increased levels of anxiety, caused by her random visits, have brought about a seismic change in my office organisation. My filing system, no, filing regime, has pushed me to an extreme of compulsive behaviour too embarrassing to reveal to anyone. Before and after work, I *have* to go through my files, in a set order, to check I have dotted every i, and crossed every t. I try to do this when the office is empty because a) I don't want anyone to see me, and b) if interrupted, I have to start the process all over again.

It is wearing, but it has to be done because she loves nothing more than to catch me out.

'Still here then,' is her opening remark as she enters my office, placing her handbag on the chair in front of my desk before removing her cream leather gloves, pulling them off one finger at a time, then laying them across her bag. I am yet to see her in the same outfit twice and today she reveals a fitted cream suit – designer, obviously – as she shrugs off her coat with its flamboyant fake fur collar and hangs it on my coat stand. She makes an infinitesimal tweak to the position of the air freshener on my shelf, as though it personally affronts her feng shui, before finally taking the other seat opposite me. She fixes me with a glare from eyes that mirror those of her son. It appears she is basing herself in my office for the duration, then. Joy.

'Still here, Mrs Marchant,' I answer, as I gaze past her to see Rex stop and share a word or two with Phil Baxter, our most recently recruited project manager. His face breaks into a smile at something Phil says and his whole demeanour changes with it. Relaxed, his usual scowl disappears and he looks like the young man he is. I can see why Sharon thinks he's handsome and it's a shame he rarely shows this side of himself.

'Not found a position elsewhere then?' She obviously believes I am job-seeking. 'It's probably your age. You should do something about the grey.' *Bitch.* She isn't too far behind me in years, although admittedly looks it. A facelift per decade will do that.

I smile sweetly. 'How may I help you this morning?'

What follows is a test of endurance as she raises her questions, written on a pad taken from her handbag and no doubt concocted with her son. These range from who earns what within the staff, through which projects are at what stage regarding their delivery, and on to which suppliers we use and what proof I have they are the most cost effective. It is mostly a lesson in me proving myself. I give her all the answers she needs, and more, adding in all the detail I can manage in an attempt to bore her so she'll leave. As though in a duel I parry each thrust she makes and it gives me immense satisfaction when she raises nothing I don't have an answer for. However, throughout her time here my heart beats fast enough in my chest for me to feel it, my breaths are shallow and my stomach squirms in fear that maybe, just maybe, the next question will be the one which catches me out.

At one point, to my horror, she clicks her fingers in Fiona's direction (*clicks her fingers!*) and tells her to get her a coffee. Fiona kindly brings me one at the same time and raises her eyebrows at me in solidarity with my situation.

When I have the opportunity with the questions she asks, I broach topics of concern with her. By my reasoning, if she wants to be involved, then she should be fully involved. The falling profits? 'Oh, Rex is on top of it all. He's told me there's plenty of work coming in.' *Has he?* The flirtation with staff? 'It'll be a fling. She's *only* a receptionist.' *As if that makes it perfectly acceptable then.* The inappropriate spend on the credit card? 'Oh well, boys will be boys,' followed by an overindulgent chuckle.

I have no idea what colour the sky is in her world, because she is one of *those* mothers. One of the ones who turn a blind eye to each of their precious little darling's faults. And one of the ones who will defend their cherub to the end of the earth, no matter the crime. *Bullying?* Written off as a bit of horseplay.

Calling staff out of hours? That just shows his dedication to his work. *Lying?* Such creativity. I never know what he's going to surprise me with next. And so on.

From her side of things, there are the constant snipes. Mostly about her husband and me.

When I'd mentioned the flirtation issues with Rex, she'd said, 'She won't be the first to lie on her back in order to work her way up the company.' Then she gave me a look, which made the implication clear. It annoyed me that heat rose in my cheeks despite my innocence.

I hate being accused, even indirectly, of something I didn't do.

I've tried to give her the benefit of the doubt over the years. It must be difficult for wives whose husbands work long hours in the company of other women, and yes, some do have affairs. But we hadn't, so I would have appreciated the same consideration from her.

Eventually, she rises to leave shortly before lunch, and my heart rises in unison. 'Oh, going so soon?' The words pop out of my mouth and I don't even attempt to stop them. She ignores me, visits Rex's office briefly, then walks out without further word. Rude woman.

Friday afternoon, the office phone rings, the sound interrupting my focus on the spreadsheet in front of me. I gaze through the glass wall of my office and across to reception. There is no one at the desk. Rolling my eyes at the youth of today who abandon their post at the first opportunity, I lift the handset from its cradle in my office and answer.

'Marchant & Son, how may I help you?' Mr Marchant Senior would have appreciated the familiar greeting, something I'd fought tooth and nail to keep. No automated messages here, thank you. No press this, hold the line, choose how to direct your call nonsense either. Straight through to a human, as I prefer it myself.

'Hello, can I have your accounts department, please?'

'Speaking, I'm Alice Fraser. How can I help?'

'Ah, I wasn't expecting you to answer the phone.' The relief shows in his voice as he continues, 'It's Tony Scampton here. I wanted to get your bank details. Rex has asked me to transfer a deposit and I need to get it set up as I'm off on holiday for a month and don't want to mess around with this while I'm away.' I am aware of the Scampton account. The extensive oak-framed farmhouse Marchant & Son is due to build. Although I don't like Rex's new policy of asking for a substantial deposit upfront. What is wrong with payments in line with the structural engineer's reports? Then, I have to remind myself, this is the new regime and Tony Scampton is a friend of Rex's. If Rex has talked him into the deposit, then that's the way it has to be. Although I have a horrible feeling he will have given him a discount, too. Being a mate and all.

'Of course.' I reel off the account details. Tony reads them back to confirm they are correct.

'I have a limit of fifty thou a day at the bank, so I'll send the full two hundred K over four days from the thirteenth to the sixteenth, if you could let Rex know?' I understood, we have the same limit on our bank account too.

'Yes, of course, I'll pass on the message and monitor the funds coming into our bank. Thank you for your business.'

'You're welcome, love. Rex is a good mate, and the company has a great reputation, so we have high expectations.'

'And we shall look forward to meeting them. Thank you for your call, and have a lovely holiday.'

'I'm sure we will, love, cheers,' he says, and hangs up. Fancy having the wherewithal to transfer such a large amount of money. And it is only the deposit. Mind you, imagine going off on holiday for a month, too.

It's interesting that, like with Sharon, he sees a different side of Rex than I do. But I've found that is often the case with the outside world.

The door to the main office swings open. I look over to see Rex enter along with Trish, the receptionist. I know she was here during her lunch break so they haven't arrived back together, but clearly he was the one to lure her away from her desk. Trish is a young woman of twenty who shows potential and who I am hoping to train into a more inspiring role. I don't like the way Rex leers at her, nor his wolfish grin. The way she gazes back at him is problematic, too. *Tsk*. I can feel another recruitment drive being added to my to-do list. Maybe I've been mistaken in thinking she could climb higher in the company after all. As Rex passes by the open door to my corner office, I call out to him.

'Tony Scampton rang.' He breaks his stride and does at least turn back to stick his head round my open door.

'And?' He's been drinking. I can see the flush in his cheeks, his eyes glassy. No doubt his BMW will be outside too, he having driven back from whatever pub where he's spent the last few hours.

'He said he'd be paying his deposit over the four days be—'
He cuts me off with a dismissive wave of his hand.

'Why would that be of any interest to me?' He continues on
to his larger office in the opposite corner to mine, the glass walls
of which he'd had filled in as soon as he took over. His door
slams behind him.

When Mr Marchant Senior and I designed the current office
space, it was with organisation and efficiency in mind. The
ground floor is a display area so clients can see examples of
different materials and finishes for themselves. Our offices are
on the first floor of the building and as his heart lay toward the
building side of the business, his windows overlook the yard
and The Lodge. Mine overlook the car park.

Mr Marchant Senior's office was naturally larger than mine
and included an area which housed a table and chairs so he
could meet and talk with potential clients in a more relaxed
manner. Proper coffee and biscotti would be served, sometimes
a buffet lunch. Mr Marchant Senior was welcoming, but
preferred things to be kept businesslike.

In Rex's time he's brought in a drinks cabinet, which he
indulges in whether clients are present or not, sometimes
inviting female employees in to join him. Then the rest of the
staff get treated to giggles along with any other sounds that
emanate from the room, which makes everyone uncomfortable.
I also heard him mention to one woman, who has since left, his
plan to bring in a pool table and get rid of the client area
altogether. I have no idea if he was joking or not, finding him
rather lacking in any sense of humour, unless the crude jibes he
makes are what pass for one in his case.

I wait until the door to his office closes before shaking my head, ignoring him and his comment, which is what I do when he's been drinking. I have enough to do anyway because on the desk before me sits my nemesis, which brings its own daily problems and was introduced by Rex with no prior discussion or planning. One Monday morning, I'd walked into the office to find the upgraded computer system in place. I suppose, grudgingly, the machines we had been using were past their best, and no doubt behind the times and, to be fair, discussions had already begun about their replacement. But the system Rex had brought in, sold by one of his mates, is a giant step too far. Or perhaps I am simply too old to take all the changes on board.

Apparently, it's intuitive. Whatever that might mean. The youngsters in the office certainly find it easier to learn, and I feel my age every time I have to ask for help. The problem is there is no instruction manual. Which is what I prefer. A decent-sized volume I can open on my desk to refer to in times of difficulty. But no, with this system, I have to seek any help I need online, and it doesn't come naturally. Particularly not when my confidence is at such a low ebb, anyway.

Rex has also instigated, without asking, my switch over to online accounting software I simply hate. I can see no need for the change, my old system having been perfectly adequate for many years. But change is coming, he's told me, digital change, and I have to move with it, or I will no longer be of any use to the company.

Message received loud and clear.

The old girl's past it.

I hate how paranoid he's made me, but remain convinced he's carried out all these changes to unnerve me. Everything is done in his drive to push me out. Because, of course, I know it's what he wants me to do. Walk. Rather than he have to make me redundant. I've been there so long that to do so would cost a packet. But he's underestimated how tenacious I can be. There is no way I am going to walk and give him what he wants without receiving what is rightfully mine. Absolutely no way.

I have to admit at first I was amazed at Rex's initiative in getting the new system installed and running, even if the planning for such an upgrade was lacking. I'd been hopeful this was a positive move towards him becoming more involved with the company. No such luck. The computer system switch is the only thing he has invested his energy into for the business, and I am sure it was only to impress his friend. He certainly did nothing to impress anyone he employed.

At appraisal time, there were no salary increases, no bonuses. He cancelled the summer barbeque. There was nothing even at Christmas, not so much as a party popper, let alone a party. Mr Marchant Senior had taken all the staff out to a local restaurant for dinner. Hired out the whole place and brought in a disco for dancing afterwards. Partners invited.

And it isn't only me who struggles with the change in management. Rex undermines and belittles all those around him, which I am sure is what is behind the increase in staff turnover. All those who've left were conscientious, all talented, all went seeking brighter futures elsewhere. I can't blame them, but it bothers him not one jot. There'll always be others, is his way of thinking. Always someone with their hand out wanting me to support their family, he's said, and I loathe this disrespectful view he has of those who work hard for him.

I've also noticed there is no *we* any more. *We*, is a thing of the past. Now, it is only *I*. Mr Marchant Senior had made me feel we were in this together and this change isolates me more than ever.

Rex has hardly been in his office for ten minutes before he walks out again. As he passes my door, he slows briefly, but without making eye contact says, 'I'm off.'

I make a point of looking at my watch, but say nothing. I am used to him ducking out early on a Friday.

A short while later, I call Trish into my office and ask her to close the door because this could be a tricky conversation. It is one I should have had with other staff but hadn't done so early enough and had lost them. I'm not about to let it happen again. She perches on the edge of the chair, her eyes wide.

'Don't worry, Trish, you've done nothing wrong. But you've been with us for a while now, and I wanted to have a word about your work. How are you finding it? Are you coping with what you've been given all right?' She visibly relaxes.

'Oh, okay. I thought I was in trouble.'

'Of course you're not. I'm pleased with your work. But how are you feeling about it?' She smiles for the first time.

'I'm enjoying working here. I like the variety and there's plenty to keep me busy.'

'Good. And, are you getting on all right with everyone? Any issues I should know about?' She hesitates for a moment, focuses on her hands in her lap.

'No, I think I'm settling in fine. Not that I really know anyone here, yet.' This is alarming in itself because I've seen it before, and again had acted too late. Rex has a habit of playing favourites and singles out his chosen ones, always women, which means others in the firm ostracise them because they are worried about what might get back to their boss. 'Has someone said something?'

'No. No one's said anything. But I can't help noticing Rex distracts you a lot.' Colour rises in her cheeks.

'I know, but I get my work done. I make sure of it.'

'I'm sure you do. But it's not the point. Do you feel uncomfortable with the way he treats you?'

'A little. I mean, he's attractive and everything, but with him being my boss…'

'He's hard to say no to?'

'Exactly.' She is relieved I understand.

'You might find this next question awkward, Trish. But has he put you under any pressure to do him any sexual favours?'

'No.' She threads her fingers together and has difficulty meeting my eyes. 'Not really.'

'Not really?' She tilts her head to one side then the other as though trying to decide whether to say anything further.

'He called me the other night. I think he'd been drinking. He made a suggestion he said could earn me a bonus.' I have to force myself not to tut.

'Okay. Well, none of that is appropriate, Trish. Not the calling you after hours and certainly not the suggestion. I'm sorry this has happened. The flirting while you're at work is also wrong.'

'I don't know how to stop him.'

'I understand, but leave it with me. I'll have a word with him.'

'No, please don't do that. He'll sack me.' Her eyes widen and I can see the panic in them.

'In which case sue him for wrongful dismissal.' My words are stern, and I know she wasn't expecting such a robust response. 'I'm not messing about, Trish. This behaviour of his has to stop. Besides, I do the hiring and firing around here.' I smile to ensure she realises I am on her side. 'In the meantime, don't take his calls and I suggest you ignore his behaviour at work by not reacting when he comes on to you. Hopefully, it won't be an issue again, anyway, as I'll speak to him the next chance I get.'

She leaves my office shortly after, hopefully with more confidence than when she'd entered it, while I am left to ponder what I now have to face. I know I can deal with difficult situations. Staffing issues. Contract negotiations. Tricky clients. They might challenge me, but I am experienced and can find my way through to an adequate solution. So why is it the mere suggestion of having to confront Rex on anything makes my heart palpitate? I can feel it now. A lightening sensation in my chest. I take a deep breath, then another. The anticipation of what I'm going to have to face causes a roll of nausea through my stomach. Goodness only knows what state I'll be in when Rex is right in front of me. And I have the entire weekend to get through first.

4: Clean-Ups and Break-Ins

I usually spend Saturday morning having coffee and cake with Dora, but this week I plan to clean her cottage in readiness for her return. I take the key I hold for emergencies off its hook and go to get started, totally unprepared for the sight that greets me. Our other friends, Sally Button and Susannah Bugby, had been in the cottage briefly on the night of the Murder Mystery. We were in touch over the last week organising who was going to do what and they'd mentioned it was in a bit of a state, but they were being kind. Or hadn't seen the full extent of the mess.

It has been a few weeks since I was last round at Dora's and everything had appeared normal then, but Dora's world had obviously careered out of control since. I stand in the doorway to the kitchen, my nose wrinkling at the smell. Dirty crockery and glasses line the worktops and table. Grey fur grows on ready meal containers tossed in the grimy sink. The few items in the fridge are mouldy, vegetables rotting to soggy lumps in their packaging, other items so far out of date even I can no longer trust them. And there are wine bottles everywhere. Mostly empty.

The sitting room has paperwork strewn across each piece of furniture and the floor, piles of it. Dust lies thick on every surface, cobwebs crowd corners and loop from ceiling to light fixtures. The carpet is gritty beneath my feet as rolls of fluff gather along skirtings. I kick myself for not thinking there was something wrong the last time I tried to come round. That Saturday when Dora had barely cracked the door open, having supposedly overslept, then suggested we meet at my house instead. It is obvious now what she was hiding. But then why would I have suspected anything? I've known Dora for years. She is the most together person I know. I sigh as I turn back to the kitchen.

I'd arranged for Sally and Susannah to come round late morning but want to get the worst of it done before they get here.

Leaving the back door open to air the place, I take the bottles out to the recycling bin, then clean out the fridge. I wash up, dry and put everything away. Then I wipe the worktops and kitchen table, scrubbing its surface to remove the wine stains. I collect all the notepads and scraps of paper together in the sitting room while averting my eyes. I don't read a word, but the large photos of Amos Chamberlain taken while he was out and about around the village are hard to ignore.

I know he is under investigation by the police for what he did to Dora and I'm sure he'll face charges. How can he not? There was no lack of witnesses to the assault. He's already resigned from the Parish Council and Village Hall Committee, and from what I've heard, no one has seen him since the Murder Mystery. Good riddance to him. Dora had fallen into a dark place and it was hard to believe what she went through. In time, maybe she will talk to me about it.

Once the paperwork is in one tidy pile, I attack the cobwebs with a feather duster, then dust the surfaces, followed by vigorously vacuuming throughout downstairs before washing the kitchen floor.

Doing something physical is such a change to my day job, it gives me plenty of thinking time. While my anger had spiked with the reminder of Amos, my mind remains concentrated on my work issues, the combined stress providing me with plenty of energy to burn off by channelling it into my thorough cleaning session.

Marchant & Son, Mr Marchant Senior being the original son, is a building company that builds houses throughout three counties and he had proudly taken on the small company and developed it into a sizeable concern.

He'd had grand plans for the future too, plans he'd shared with me with tremendous enthusiasm. Again, I'd imagined it was because he didn't get the support to do so at home, although maybe I flattered myself. He'd ensured his developments provided a mix of housing, rather than only including larger houses with the best profit margins. But now the company was of a certain size, he wanted to make considerably more effort to provide affordable starter homes, going so far as to set up a housing association to make access to housing possible for all. Under this umbrella, his altruistic side flourished as he'd also drawn up plans to build a community to get those living on the streets into a home of their own. I remembered his excitement when he'd shown me how he'd seen the future, and naively I'd seen it as my duty to help Mr Marchant Junior guide the company into continuing in the direction his father had set it on.

But Rex was having none of it. What had followed had been nothing short of disappointment after disappointment. Mr Marchant Junior showed none of his father's brilliance or generosity. Instead I witnessed a selfish young man make it clear he had no interest in the business other than for it to continue to make money for him to spend. And as though he was determined to prove just how unlike his father he was, bit by bit he changed everything about the company his father had made good. The housing association was closed down without a moment's hesitation.

This, what I saw as a backward step for the company, broke my heart. I'd never considered it before, but with no husband, no children and no other family to care for, this was it. My baby. My responsibility. I knew it wasn't. I had no stake in it other than emotionally, but that's how it was. That was why I'd accepted whatever additional tasks or responsibilities Mr Marchant Senior had asked of me. Until, and this was what saved my job when Rex stepped in, I was as firmly woven into the fabric of the company as the bricks and mortar that provided the structure it was based in. Abigail was no fool.

I find it cathartic to thump the sofa cushions, imagining they have Rex and Abigail's faces on them, and by the time I finish I doubt they've ever been plumper.

I am glad I kept the back door open as it's hot work and I appreciate the cool, fresh air as it flows through the cottage. I'd taken the vacuum and all the cleaning products upstairs when there is a knock on the front door. Sally and Susannah are on the doorstep, insulated freezer boxes in each of their hands, but before any of us can utter a word, the back door slams with the through draught. I jump at the sound, then turn back to my friends to welcome them in.

'Thanks for coming. I've washed the kitchen floor so can you leave those in there while it dries?' I point to the sitting room.

'What can we do?' Susannah casts her eye round the room. 'Have you already finished?'

'I haven't touched upstairs yet, so you could help me there.' I lead the way and between the three of us, we make quick work of the bedrooms and bathroom.

Sally strips Dora's bed, collects the towels and takes all the dirty laundry downstairs to load into the washing machine, later. I want to have everything washed, dried, and put away before she gets back. Susannah remakes the bed and while she cleans Dora's room, Sally does the spare room and I tackle the bathroom.

When we come downstairs, the kitchen floor has dried so Sally and Susannah begin unloading their boxes into the fridge and freezer while I go to get us each a coffee from my cottage. When I get back, they've finished, having stocked the fridge with fresh vegetables, milk and cheese, plus a couple of home-cooked vegetarian dishes. The freezer is full of meals to keep Dora going for a while.

'Oops, I nearly forgot something,' I say, and dash over to my cottage to retrieve a tablecloth, to cover what remains of the wine stains, and a vase of flowers I'd bought to place on Dora's table. While we drink our coffee, we toast our efforts.

As we'd worked, there had been little conversation beyond what we were doing. Now we are sitting drinking coffee, the chat turns to what brought us here.

'How bad is the gossip in the village?' I say, my job keeping me out of circulation.

'It's already petering out, don't you think?' Sally asks Susannah, who nods.

'Yes, it is. I think people are sympathetic and don't want to keep talking about her. Although, of course, Sharon has been all over it, as you can imagine. Gutted not to have witnessed the incident, she's more than made up for it since. Raking over every detail.'

'I can imagine. I only popped into the shop briefly and she mentioned it then.'

'I can't believe Amos and Dora kept their past a secret all these years,' says Susannah.

'Do you think Evelyn knew about it?' asks Sally.

'She must have done, surely,' I reply, then raise my mug. 'Here's to Dora, getting home soon and recovering quickly.' We tap our mugs together.

The next day, I receive a call from Eddie Lumbers.

'Sorry to call you on a Sunday. There's been a break-in at the yard which I'll deal with but thought you should know about.'

'Not again. How irritating. A lot taken?' This happens occasionally, an occupational hazard. Thieves are always eager to find out what we keep in the building, and leave a long enough gap between burglaries for us to have replaced the items they stole the last time they were there.

'Nothing hugely expensive, mostly smaller tools. It's more the damage caused that's the nuisance. I'm heading over there now to do some repairs and replace the locks.'

'Thank you. Have you called the police? Or do you want me to do it?'

'No, it's done, but they don't know when they'll get out.' This is the standard response we get nowadays, and it's rare for someone to be caught, but we have to call to get a crime number to claim on the insurance.

'What about the CCTV? Anything useful on there?'

'I've got it to show to the police. Three culprits. Dressed in black, faces covered. The usual. I'm not sure what use it will be for them.'

'And Rex?'

'I'm about to phone him next, although I daresay he'll hate me for interrupting his Sunday.' I smile. He's not wrong, although Rex will take it better from Eddie, and I'm glad he is the one making the call. Interesting that Rex is the last one either of us consider contacting.

5: Whistle-blower

'I need to talk to you,' I blurt out to Rex as he passes my office door. My voice is stronger than I feel. I may have barely slept and been nauseous all weekend in the build-up to this confrontation, but my annoyance at him rolling into the office at noon has at least fuelled my determination to tackle him head on.

He doubles back, sighs loudly and makes no effort to cover his irritation.

'What do you want?'

'It's about Trish.' He lifts his hand to stop me immediately.

'I'm not dealing with any of this shit. I'm going out to lunch.' And as easily as that, he swerves the conversation in another direction.

'But you've only just arrived.'

'My company, my rules. Besides, this is networking. All done to keep you in a fucking job so you could at least be grateful.'

'Will you be coming back to the office later?'

'I'm only going as far as the golf club to check on the build there so I should think so. Why, is it likely I'll be needed?' Sarcasm laces his sullen tone as he walks off to his office.

As it happens, no, he won't, but that isn't the point. He is supposed to be in charge and his constant absences take their toll on getting things done. "To check on the build there", is a joke too. It is nothing more than a feeble reason he's added in an attempt to justify his whereabouts. What does matter is I now know where he is going to be over the next little while, and what he'll be doing.

It is time to put some pressure on Rex.

For a while, I've had a plan forming to bring some trouble into his life and this last piece of the jigsaw, the opportunity piece, has just fallen into place. Yes, it is mischievous of me. I hesitate to use the word wicked, and yes, I am probably being petty, but a person can only take so much and I have taken far more than anyone should. Besides, what I have planned for him might also wake him up to what he is doing and the risk he poses to others. Although he's so self-obsessed, I doubt it.

The build at the golf club he is apparently so interested in, is to add a small property for use by the grounds person there. Eddie Lumbers is the site foreman for the project, so I call him.

'Hi, Alice, how are you?'

'I'm fine, and you?'

'A day in the open air is always a good one, you know that.' I can hear the smile in his oft-repeated words. Eddie is an excellent leader of men and great in a managerial role, but I know he prefers being on site to being inside dealing with paperwork. 'How can I help?'

'I called to tell you Rex is lunching at the golf club today.'

'Good to know, thank you. Not that the team is slacking, of course, but with the big boss man checking in, I shall make sure he's given a guided tour.'

That will be the last thing Rex will want, which only makes Eddie's suggestion more appealing. 'Please do and make sure it's a long one. I know he'll appreciate every minute it'll take.' I laugh lightly and can hear Eddie chuckle.

'Don't worry, I'll be thorough, but doubt I'll be able to keep him from his gin and tonic for too long. I'll return the favour and let you know when he's heading back.'

'Thank you.'

Before I get back to work I check then double-check the second, and as yet unused, mobile I carry in my bag. The one I bought to execute this plan. It is charged and ready for use. Not long after, Rex walks out of his office, leaving without a word to me or anyone else. His BMW exits the car park and the time from that moment on slows to a sloth's crawl and I have to force myself not to keep checking the clock. I carry on working as I eat lunch at my desk, although concentrating on any task is a challenge. My mobile startles me when it rings at three-thirty, despite the fact I've been expecting it every minute since Rex left.

'Hello.'

'Hi, I can report the big boss man thoroughly enjoyed his tour and has no doubt had a terrific lunch. He's walking to his car now.'

'Thanks for letting me know. We shall stand by for his arrival. Speak to you soon.' I don't need to alert anyone to his approach, because, of course, we are getting our work done. But I stand and close my office door.

I take the second mobile from my handbag, turn to look out of the window, and make a call before opening the door again.

From then on, it takes every ounce of willpower to not keep watch on the car park.

I knew his "networking" lunch would be a long one. They always were. I knew he would drink. He always does. I know, despite that, he will drive back to the office. Because he is a selfish man who doesn't give a damn about anyone's life other than his own.

He is also arrogant enough to believe he is untouchable.

I try to guess how long it will take for him to get back to the office without any interruptions to his journey. And then if he happens to be held up.

My heart sinks when I discover I am astonishingly accurate with my first guess as I see him arrive back in the car park. Initially disappointed, my hopes then lift along with my heartbeat, as I spot a police car follow him in. It pulls up alongside his BMW. The two officers approach Rex as he is getting out.

Over the time I've spent working for him, I've become adept at reading his body language. Now challenged, he swiftly becomes belligerent, throwing his arms around, which is no surprise to me. He doesn't hold his drink well. The officers remain calm and professional as they try to reason with him. Although my money would have been on him refusing a test, his arrogance clearly overrides any sense he might have had when sober and makes him believe he will pass as a short while later he is blowing into a breathalyser. I have everything crossed that for once in his life he hasn't gone against form.

I'm not to be disappointed. Rex's fury is easy to spot even at this distance.

Fascinated to see what happens next, I can't look away but make sure I am far enough back from the window that should he glance up, he won't spot me. This allows me to be treated to the pleasure of watching him being put into the back of the police car and driven away.

I wasn't the only one who witnessed what occurred. When I finally tear my gaze away from the window, several members of staff, Fiona and Phil included, are standing by their desks and peering out at the unexpected show put on for them. Fiona raises her eyebrows at me as she turns back to her work and we both have a faint smile on our lips.

After such excitement, it is tough to settle back at my desk. My mind keeps wandering off to what is going on at the police station. I'm not sure of the process or whether Rex will face charges or be let go, and irritatingly it might be something I'll never find out, as he is hardly likely to broadcast it. I am sure the other staff are as unsettled as I am by what happened, so I'm glad the afternoon is nearly over and I'm soon locking up for the night and on my way home.

My plan to bring some trouble into Rex's life has been bubbling away in my mind for a while. Petty revenge, I guess you'd call it. I hadn't known when, or even if, I'd get the opportunity to mess with him, but I'd made sure I was ready, just in case. Anonymous calls are not something I do regularly though, so I feel uneasy as I drive home. So uneasy, in fact, I take a long route back to Melton in order to dispose of the mobile I'd used, in several bins along the way. It was a flip phone, and I'd broken it in half, then cut the SIM card in two. Of course, I had been cautious and worn vinyl gloves before wiping each part, to remove fingerprints, prior to dumping it. It is way over the top for what I've done, but I can't afford to be discovered as the whistle-blower on Rex's drink driving. My job hangs by a thread as it is.

I was similarly careful when I bought the mobile. Months ago, when my car was in the garage, Sally Button offered to drive me into town and I took the opportunity. I'd left my mobile at home so my provider would assume I was there, should anyone ever check. I'd paid in cash and because it was raining, it was acceptable for me to have my hood up to hide my identity from any cameras. Although, at my age I am obviously invisible anyway, especially to the young things selling the tech.

Since then, the mobile has lain in my bag charged but switched off, waiting for the opportunity to use it. It is a terrific waste of money, for one call, but I don't dare keep it for fear of getting caught.

I have to admit I had rather enjoyed planning the subterfuge. What had started out as little more than a daydream had mushroomed into a properly laid-out and considered plan. And it was something a bit different that had brought some excitement to my otherwise steady life. But now I've done the deed, I'm uncomfortable; it is as though I am the one in the wrong and it leaves me feeling unsettled.

Once my front door is closed behind me, I let out a long-held breath. As I walk through to the kitchen, I say, 'George, you're not going to believe what I did today.' Yes, I am aware there is no one but me in the house. And, no, I am not mad. I know my husband is dead. But I still talk to him, I always have. Even after all these years. Although, obviously, I keep it within the four walls of my home so as not to alarm people.

When you become a widow or widower, it leaves you dangling, which is something a lot of people don't think about. I couldn't work out my feelings at the time it happened, couldn't understand them. But unlike when a marriage breaks down and there's a process the couple goes through when one, or both, slowly attempt to fall out of love with the other, when it's death that separates you, it's a relationship interrupted, and the love is left but has nowhere to go.

I learned this while thumbing through a magazine one day while in the dentist's waiting room. The article was actually about online dating, the delights and dangers thereof. It's not something I would ever put myself through, but felt intrigued enough to read it. Then I was shocked to discover one warning was: *Don't date a widow or widower. Unless, of course, you're a masochist and want to go out with someone who is still in love with someone else*. Put out by the article at the time, I dismissively believed it to be a bit of a generalisation as I was sure there were plenty of bereaved people out there only too happy to be rid of their other halves without having to go through the faff of divorcing them, and they'd have had no problem dating again. But the article had stayed with me and as time went on, I understood it more and more because George and I had been terribly in love. And I'd never been sure how you fell out of love with a dead person. It felt unfair somehow to do so, as though you were leaving them behind. And I didn't think I could sleep with someone else and not feel I was cheating. I did acknowledge, however, that my need to keep chatting to George had possibly been instrumental in my never having had another relationship because I hadn't even tried to move on.

And no, I should add for clarification, he doesn't reply.

But he is a great sounding board. I frequently discuss my problems with him. Okay, at him. Often, by the time I've talked it all out, the solution has presented itself. What can I say? It works for me, and it helps me feel a little less lonely.

Occasionally I hear, deep inside, the response I know he would give in a certain situation. Which always makes me smile.

Besides seeking the sanctuary of my home, I was also keen to get back today as Dora was to be discharged and, although I knew Susannah Bugby was going to bring her home, I want to ensure she is settled in. What I need before doing anything further, though, is a strong cup of tea. While I make it, I update George on what I've done, hoping saying it out loud to him will settle my nerves. And, while I can imagine his satisfied chuckle at the result I've achieved, my hands still shake as I hold the kettle under the tap. Perhaps skulduggery doesn't come as naturally to me as I thought.

I know, were he here, George would have given me a stern talking-to and would have told me not to worry as I can't do anything to change the situation, but I continue to dwell on it, so to distract myself I go over to knock on Dora's back door. I'm delighted when she answers and, despite my protestations that I only want to check she is home safely, she invites me in. Dora has recently made a pot of tea, so we sit at her kitchen table to enjoy a cup and she thanks me for sorting out the house and food so beautifully for her. I brush away her thanks as it is only what anyone would do for their friend and neighbour.

She is coping with her arm in plaster and I'm pleased to see the bruising around her jaw has improved vastly from when I first saw her. She assures me the rest of her wounds are healing, too.

'Eddie asked me to pass on his regards to you.'

A twinkle comes to her eyes for the first time. 'That is kind. Been spending time with him, have you?'

'No, he was cleaning my car.'

'Ooh, he's trying to get in your good books, then.' She smiles, though with the swelling it is lopsided, but still good to see. I know she'd love nothing more than for me to find romance, and she's mentioned Eddie as a possible on more than one occasion.

I can tell she is stronger already and more focused. But she still comes across as subdued to me, which I guess is what you'd expect and, although I am keen to ask about her mental health, I don't want to pry. Eventually, she volunteers the information that she started counselling while in the hospital. Apparently, the doctors feel it will be the most beneficial course of treatment for her and when I ask how it's going, she says, 'So far, so good.'

I leave after twenty minutes. She knows where I am if she needs anything and we've decided to resume our Saturday morning coffee and cake chats so we'll catch up then. As I am leaving though, she says the strangest thing, 'There have been phone calls you know. Several of them. But whoever it was did not leave a message.'

'Okay,' I say, not exactly sure of the significance. Although she is unfazed by this response, I wander home perplexed and, after what has happened, more than a little worried that perhaps she isn't ready to come home after all.

The visit to see Dora has been a distraction, but once home I get back to thinking about my Rex problem, while at the same time hoping I'm not becoming obsessed with the situation, as I've seen what obsession had done to Dora. Whatever doubts I had earlier about my suitability to a life of crime, I am calmer by the time I prepare supper and can't help a smile coming to my face because, however bad it made me feel about myself, the outcome of my meddling today has also given me a certain amount of pleasure. The vision of Rex getting into the back of the police car is one I'll cherish for a while.

Today's mischief-making isn't the only plan that has sprung from little more than a daydream, either. Rex's behaviour has caused me to have many others bubbling in my mind. Some are simply daydreams and best left at that. I have no desire to spend the rest of my days in prison. Some have the potential to bring minor instances of misery into his life. Others… well, others are of another level entirely and are coming together to make a more cohesive idea of what could be possible. One of these ideas has come from a memory dredged up from decades ago and is considerably more audacious than all the others. But I am unconvinced I possess the level of cunning required to execute it successfully. Though if not me, then who?

To protect my future, it is important nothing is traced back to me, in case it all goes wrong. Therefore, once I've eaten, I sit with the plans contained only in my head and go through the details again, running them past George as though seeking his approval until I am satisfied I am still safe. All I have to do now is remain patient. If it is meant to be, like today, my opportunity will present itself.

6: Spectator Gold

Some days are simply golden, and this turns out to be one of them. By some glorious serendipity, the stars have aligned. Or, more likely, the checks by the police the previous day have expedited matters. Which means I am outside in the car park when Rex arrives in his mother's car late the next morning, his mother in the driver's seat. I sign the docket on the clipboard handed to me by the flatbed truck driver and give it back to him. His colleague has already wrapped the towing chains around the front wheels of Rex's BMW and is hauling it up the ramp and onto the back of the flatbed. Unfortunately for Rex, this action has drawn a crowd as everyone has come out to watch the spectacle.

'Hey, stop!' Rex, panicked, leaves the car door open and runs across to the driver. 'What are you doing with my car?'

'Been repossessed, mate,' the driver says, before heading back to the cab.

'Don't be ridiculous. And don't "mate" me. Unload it right now.' Etched into every word is his entitlement, as is his public school accent.

'Can't do that, *sir*.' He opens the door and makes to climb in.

Rex turns to me. 'What do they mean, repossessed?'

Abigail, immaculate as ever in a sky blue shift dress and jacket along with the obligatory matching heels, joins us on the pavement. 'What's going on?'

I am happy to provide a summary. 'According to their paperwork, Rex has been driving uninsured. The lender has obtained a court order and now they're taking the car back as he's breached their conditions.'

'There's obviously been a mistake,' Abigail says, because naturally her son can't possibly have done anything wrong, 'anyway,' and she pounces on an opportunity to lay the blame, 'don't you deal with all that?'

'I used to but Rex prefers to do it himself nowadays, said my work was, what was it, Rex? That's it, "shoddy", because apparently he didn't like the company I'd insured him with.'

'But I did it, I did sort it out, I haven't been driving uninsured.' Despite coming across as though he is a spoilt child, he sounds convincing enough, although then he frowns as if second-guessing himself. 'No, it must be some mistake. I'll go in and sort it out.' He almost turns towards the office, but then gazes longingly back at his car, his arms outstretched, as if he can't quite bring himself to leave it. 'My car…'

'There's little you can do about it now,' I say rather callously then, distracted, add, 'Oh, the police are here.' This refocuses Rex on the possibility of preventing the imminent departure of his beloved car.

'Good, perhaps they can stop these thieving bastards.' As he walks off towards the officers, every employee remains solidly in place, no one keen to miss the next part of the drama.

Abigail leans in closer and says, 'What have you done?'

'Nothing,' I say, and I meet her raptor eyes without hesitation before I add, 'and I'm offended you would think I had.'

Rex is gesticulating wildly towards his car, in case the officers can't see it. 'Do something. My car's being stolen and I need you to stop them.'

The older of the two, with barely a tilt of his head, sends the other off to the cab to speak to the driver. He is handed the clipboard, and all eyes are on him as he checks through the paperwork. Apparently satisfied, he hands the clipboard back through the window, shakes his head at his partner, and the engine of the flatbed starts. There is a jolt as it pulls away. All present pause as if in suspended animation in anticipation of Rex actually shedding tears as we watch his pride and joy being carried off across the car park.

The younger officer re-joins the group, breaking the moment as he says, 'He's not insured. His lender has repossessed.'

'Oh dear, oh dear, that's not a good start. In fact, that's serious, that is. Six points on your licence and a minimum three-hundred-pound fine, and, as you've seen, your vehicle can be taken away. *If* you were the owner, it could even be destroyed.' I can't speak for everyone present, but I thoroughly enjoy how much the older officer appears to relish imparting this information.

'Destroyed!' Rex repeats, his voice strained, his eyes wide with disbelief. 'Can't you stop them?'

'Stop them? Oh no. If your lender hadn't been about to repossess, we would have done so. And what I mentioned before, it's only the start. If you get taken to court, which in this case you may well be, the fine can be unlimited and you may even get disqualified from driving. Although,' and he hesitates, 'I understand that could be something you're facing, anyway.' I can barely keep the smile from my face as the officer tuts quite distinctly. 'Do you want to know which section of the Road Traffic Act you've violated?'

'No, I bloody don't! Fucking useless, the lot of you!' His mother places a restraining hand on his forearm, but he throws it off as he rounds on the officers. 'What are you even doing here, anyway?'

'We've received a report of a burglary?'

'What! That was on Sunday! And you're only here now?'

'The thieves had already left the premises when it was reported to us, sir, so it was not an emergency.' I can sense Rex's anger is swiftly reaching boiling point and am relieved when Eddie Lumbers steps forward.

'I can deal with this. Please come this way.' He indicates towards the gateway to the side of the office block. 'I can show you what's happened. I've also sorted out a copy of the CCTV for you.'

'Thank you,' the older officer smiles and the three men take the route round to the backyard.

Rex, as if he's only then noticed this morning's activities have drawn an audience, barks at the crowd, 'Get back to work, the lot of you, what the fuck am I paying you for?' and he waves his hands in a shooing motion as if to reinforce his command.

I follow the others into the building and go straight back to my desk, trying to appear composed and not at all excited by the events of the morning.

Not long after, the main door slams as Rex storms into the building. Rage emanates from every pore as he marches past my door and disappears into his office. Even if I had an urgent question to ask him, there would be no way I would approach him now. It would be like poking an angry bear with a stick.

No one speaks as each of us concentrate on working and keeping a low profile. The tension throughout the office is palpable, such is his influence on everyone's mood. I rotate my shoulders and do some neck exercises to release the tension held there.

A few minutes later, and presumably at what she considers a safe distance, Abigail walks into reception then proceeds to his office, appearing as though there is nothing wrong.

'If I can be of any help, Mrs Marchant, do let me know,' I call out as she passes. Having about as much grace as her son, she does not reply.

As he stated outside, I assume Rex is now going to call his insurers to sort the misunderstanding out. Despite my offer he fortunately chooses not to involve me, and a short while later I, and all the others at their desks, hear him bellowing at some poor unfortunate on the other end of the phone. Moments later, silence falls. He then storms out of his office and swings through the door of mine. Leaning across my desk, he thrusts his finger furiously at me.

'Did you do this?' I turn calmly from my screen to his snarling face and try not to appear intimidated.

'Do what?'

'Cancel my direct debit.'

'Of course not. Why would I have done that?'

'To get back at me.'

'For what?' I hesitate as a glimmer of hope rears in me that maybe, in his fury, he will confess to how badly he's been treating me. But he is too sharp to reveal himself.

'I don't know, but you're always on at me for something.'

'That's because I'm trying to help you.'

'More like boss me around. I'm not having it, not from you.' You'd have imagined he'd have outgrown such petulance by his age, but apparently not. A shadow passes across his eyes as something springs to mind, and his finger is back, jabbing in my direction, 'Hang on, you do the bookkeeping. How come you didn't alert me to the fact the payments weren't going through?'

'Did you give me the documentation to set your insurer up as a creditor on our accounts?'

A flicker of uncertainty shows in the way his eyes slide away from mine. He isn't as sure of his footing now as he was with his accusation. But unable to take responsibility, he replies, 'Of course I did.'

'Shall we take a quick look?' I am aware of just how patronising I sound, which may not help his mood, but always willing to assist, especially when I am confident of my ground, I log in to the software and trace my way back to the first payment of his insurance. I check the documentation I'd attached to it. Ideally, you'd want an invoice or at least a breakdown of the payments, which would be going out each month. All I had was an email from Rex. I open the email trail and turn my screen so he can read it as easily as I can.

In the first email, he'd told me he'd set up a direct debit to pay his insurance payments and gave me a rough figure of what they would be for, along with the insurance company's name. My response had been to ask for further detail, a breakdown of the payments to be taken, how many of them there would be, and, if possible, the invoice. I didn't think I was asking for too much. His response had been to tell me not to be so fucking pedantic and to fucking get on with it. He'd told me he'd given me all I needed, and he presumed I had the experience to manage it from there on. Or did he have to get someone else in to do the bookkeeping? On reading it again, it doesn't reflect any better on him now than it did when he first sent it but while I had attached it to cover my back, he had chosen not to make any further comment or provide me with the correct paperwork.

'But only two payments went out?' he says.

'Yes, so it appears.'

'And you didn't question anything when the payments stopped? How incompetent are you?'

'Why would I? I didn't know what the total premium was. If I'd had that figure and the detail of the monthly repayments, I'd have set it up properly and I'd have noticed on the bank reconciliation if a payment hadn't gone out, as it is…' and I hold out my hands, showing the problem is not one of my making.

'You must have cancelled the direct debit then.'

'That's quite an accusation. Why would I have done?'

'To get me into trouble.'

'You're sounding paranoid, Rex.' I turn to my work, then with something to add, I face him again. 'If you cancel a direct debit, the company would usually send warning emails, possibly even something by post. Didn't you receive anything?' His eyes shift from mine again. We both know how little attention he pays to any email he receives. If it might be something tedious, he simply deletes it, unread. I've seen him do it. And as for his post, the pile lies unopened on his desk for weeks, sometimes months, at a time. He doesn't respond but stands for a moment, undecided as to what else he can challenge me on. Then, when there is nothing further, he goes to leave. 'I suggest you take it up with the bank,' I say, concentrating on my screen. I smile inside, knowing doing so would keep him occupied for the next couple of hours and would ultimately be a fruitless exercise.

In fact, three hours pass before mother and son emerge again. He is tight-lipped, his cheeks flushed, and they leave without a goodbye to anyone. I have no idea how the conversation with the bank has gone, although I could guess, but presumably he has found nothing further to attack me with, so this is him beating a retreat.

I check out of the window, rewarded by the sight of him getting into his mother's car like a small boy being picked up from school after a detention.

As I get back to work, I play a game. It's one I often try to encourage myself to have a more positive attitude towards my boss. The game consists of me pondering Rex's good points. I know there must be some, even if hidden from me. Everyone has some good points. He loves his mother. I assume. He is old enough, and rich enough to have his own place, yet he still lives at home, so they must get on. That is one good thing. He is, I know, because I've watched him turn it on, superficially charming. As Sharon only mentioned recently. And she's not an easy woman to please. But I've also witnessed him in action with clients, particularly the wives. The charm flows on and off as if controlled by a tap. And I've seen the mask settle back to the one I am used to seeing, the moment he turns away from a client. I stop myself. I am meant to be picking out his good points and have already strayed from that path. But the truth is I am struggling to come up with any more. Maybe he has pets? People who have them generally have a softer side. Maybe he supports charities? Or gives money to those living on the streets? I try to visualise any of those happening but can't reconcile the image with what I know of him. He has friends, and plenty of them. I've met some, and while they all appear as boorish as him, there must be more to them than the impression I get. It certainly proves he is popular and he does plenty of socialising, so maybe he is a good friend? A generous one, perhaps? It is a shame I don't see that side of him. Maybe it would soften the perception I have.

As I travel home later I know that, with the excitement of the morning's activities, I am going to have much to chat through with George this evening.

7: The Welcome Return of Coffee and Cake

I'm usually the first one to the office, so finding Fiona waiting in the car park when I drive in the following morning is a surprise. I'd barely slept and don't have the mental capacity to think much about it because I am on tenterhooks about whether Rex will come in. And how dark his mood will be if he does.

Everyone else arrives as normal and quickly settles into their work, but the office is noticeably quieter than usual. The hush before the coming storm. It might have been my imagination, but perhaps I'm not the only anxious one.

He arrives, eventually.

I'm aware I haven't spoken to him as I promised Trish I would. Now is perhaps not the right time, but who knows when one of those will come along and it is best to grasp the nettle. So rather than try to stop him, I follow him into his office.

'What do you want?'

'You brushed me off the other day and I still need to talk to you about Trish.'

His eyes harden as his nostrils flare, his voice harsh. 'What about her?'

'This is for her and all the others. You need to stop sexually harassing employees because you are abusing your position of power.' I've spent the last few days rehearsing what to say, trying the words out in a thousand different ways so I'd be utterly ready, but when it comes to it, my insides quake so much it surprises me I can get the words out at all.

"Where did you get that load of utter bollocks?" His voice rises to a level I know will travel outside his four walls. I keep mine calm.

'We've already lost outstanding employees because of your behaviour, Rex, and it's come to my attention you've been harassing yet another member of staff. It has to stop.'

'You stupid bitch. You're exaggerating the situation, as is she. That's not what's been happening. Can't someone even pass a friendly word with a colleague now?' I take no notice of what he calls me. Once I did, but now I'm used to it.

'It's more than a friendly word though, isn't it? Contacting employees outside work hours is abuse, Rex. Suggesting they can do something for you in order to earn a bonus is harassment.' He makes a noise somewhere between a snort and a laugh.

'You are so wrong about this. It's laughable.' Something dark passes across his face. 'I'll have you know, it was she who came on to me. Like I'd want that cheap slag. She's after my money.' His eyes glitter in triumph, as he attacks her rather than defend himself. 'A gold digger, that's what she is. Thinks she'll try it on with the boss and bring herself up in the world. I'll show her. I'll sack her. See how she likes that?' My confidence grows with each lie he tells.

'And I've told her to sue you if you do.' His eyes widen as if he can't believe what I said. 'Keep away from her and any other member of staff you take a fancy to.' He leans across his desk, his chin jutting out.

'Don't threaten me because I could make life very difficult for you.'

'You already do.' Our eyes lock as silence falls. A silence in which I don't know what will follow, which way this stand-off will go. I have overstepped, I know it, but I'm in too deep to stop. Surprisingly, it is he who blinks first.

'I'm not listening to any more of this bollocks. Get out. I have an appointment.'

I leave, shaken but relieved I've managed to get my point across. Whether he'll take any notice is another matter.

Dropping into my chair as if my legs can't hold me a moment longer, I see there is a tremor in my hands on the desk, and take a couple of deep breaths to calm myself. I have never spoken to him so bluntly before and halfway through I'd considered the distinct possibility this could be a career-ending discussion, but by that point I didn't care, as I'd committed, it needed saying.

Less than ten minutes later a man – thirties, expensive suit – walks into reception and, once Trish has called through to Rex, is shown straight to his office. As Trish comes back past my door, I ask who he is. Edward Daniels, apparently. A solicitor. He isn't the company solicitor and I can only assume he is taking on Rex's car issue. A specialist, perhaps.

'Thank you for speaking to him.' She tilts her head in Rex's direction. So his voice had carried.

'I'm sorry if you heard any of that.' She shrugs. 'Are you okay?' She nods, but without conviction. 'Try not to take any notice of what he said.' I know it's going to be difficult for her and ask if she wants to go home, but she doesn't.

She lifts her chin when she says, 'Thank you, but I just want to get on with my work now.' We exchange a smile, and I leave her to it.

Edward remains in Rex's office for over an hour and they walk out together. Rex doesn't glance in my direction. He gets into Daniels' Jaguar, and I ponder how long it will take for him to get his own car back.

Two days, as it turns out. He drives into the car park on the Thursday. Sunglasses. Smug smile. As I'm leaving for my stint at the building site. It will be interesting to know how much money he's had to throw at the situation to have such a positive outcome so quickly. No doubt I'll find out once the bills come in.

Embarrassingly, it takes me until the Friday to realise what is going on, and I love those I work with all the more when I do. Having witnessed Rex's recent aggressive behaviour towards me, they never leave me alone. As in, I am never on my own in the office when there is a chance Rex could be there. I am grateful for this level of protection as, after the repossession of his car, I'd had a terrible night's sleep. The guilty sense of pleasure I'd experienced at Rex's expense over the previous couple of days was swept aside during the darkest hours when I'd fretted the night away, catastrophising about what form his retaliation would take. It won't matter he has no proof I am behind the incident. In his mind, I am guilty; I am always guilty, and he will punish me.

I also know he has a temper. I've seen him explode with fury when things don't go his way. It was a surprise when he hadn't over his car being towed, but the police presence probably prevented it. However, I am afraid one day his punishments will become physical. It would mean him stepping over a threshold into an entirely new form of abuse, but nothing has ever held him back from crossing such boundaries in the past. Hence my lack of sleep.

Without me having to say anything, though, the staff have made sure I am never alone in the office. Fiona is waiting in the car park each morning when I arrive. When questioned, she says she is going through a bout of waking early and is earning brownie points for when she needs some time off. It seems plausible. So much so, I decide to get another set of keys copied for her.

Then there is the maintenance work. I passed a list of jobs that needed doing around the office building to Eddie a while ago. I had not expected him to carry out the repairs himself, or so soon. Yet, this is the week when, after a long day on site, he arrives to do the odd jobs. His arrival is conveniently timed to coincide with when the other staff leave.

As Rex doesn't keep normal office hours, there is no problem with someone being around during the few hours he does spend with us in the middle of the day, as there will always be someone in the office with me. It is the fact he has a tendency to pop in on his way out somewhere in the evening, or he'll bring someone back to impress them and ply them with drink, that causes the problem. I often work late on my own because it is easier to concentrate once everyone has gone. I have fewer distractions then and am less likely to be interrupted. This is the time Eddie covers. He also carries out many more repairs and issues than were on the original list I gave him.

If I'd noticed what everyone was doing earlier, and how I'd been inconveniencing them, I would have altered the way I worked. Kept to the same hours as everyone else but my mind has been elsewhere so when the realisation clicks at the end of the week, I am ashamed by my lack of thought. Later, though, I do have to have a smile to myself at Fiona's eternal optimism at thinking Rex would ever grace the office with his presence that early in the morning.

Coffee and cake is at my house on the Saturday. I'd told Dora I'd provide the cake, as I didn't want her worrying about anything other than getting herself over to my cottage. She still holds out a tin of shortbread to me as I open the door, that she tells me Laura Brown had brought round for her before she went off on holiday.

'How kind,' I say, as Dora sits at my kitchen table. She looks well with no sign of the bruising left. Her cheeks have filled out, the dark shadows around her eyes are fading and her hair is back in its perfect bob.

'People have been lovely. They have been popping in all week with this and that. Even young Olivia brought me some flowers.'

'Why wouldn't she? She comes across as such a caring sort of woman.'

'Yes, she does, but I think the young have more to do than fuss around an old biddy.' I bring the coffees over to the table and sit facing my friend.

'People care about you. It's obvious. How's your week been?'

She nods along as she smiles. 'Yes, it has been all right.'

'And the counselling?' I tentatively ask. I am interested, of course, but I also want us to get to a place where we are not skirting around sensitive topics. Perhaps in this next phase of our friendship, we can talk more deeply about genuine issues.

'It is going fine, although I find it difficult to talk about things I have bottled up for so long.'

'I understand. We're not good at baring our souls, are we?' She laughs lightly.

'No, nor having to think about and discuss how things make us feel.' She starts as if she'd remembered something. 'I had the police contact me.'

'What for?'

'They wanted me to know no charges were going to be brought against me.'

'Brought against you? Why would they bring charges against you?'

'I did attack Amos, Alice. They could have charged me.'

'I suppose so, but I hadn't considered for one moment that could be a possibility.' I pause. 'What about him? The police have charged him, haven't they?'

'Yes, I believe so, but I'm trying not to think about any of it. He's gone anyway.'

'Gone? Where?'

'Off to one of his daughters, I think. I'm not sure which one. I've tried not to take any notice, you know. But the van was hard to miss.'

'And how do you feel about that?' Then I put my hand over my mouth at what I'd said.

'Are you sure you're not a counsellor?' Dora laughs, and I have to join in.

'Sorry, it just came out.'

'It's fine. I feel good about it. I was apprehensive about walking out of my front door in case I saw him, but now I don't have to be. It's such a relief.'

'He's lucky to have family willing to take him in.'

'I suppose families come through in a crisis.' Frown lines furrow her brow. 'You never mention family, Alice. Do you have any?'

'No. No one.' Then to change the subject I say, 'Would you like a top-up?' and I indicate towards her mug.

'Go on then,' and she smiles as she pushes it towards me. 'And you can tell me what has been going on with you.'

8: An Unexpected Visit

Mid-morning, I hear a knock at my front door and am surprised to find Fiona Stewart on the doorstep. I'm not sure I've ever seen her out of the office before and didn't know she even knew where I lived.

'Hello, Fiona. Are you okay?' She glances up the street nervously, as though checking for someone, and I follow her gaze to see who. There is no one in sight.

'I'm fine. Sorry about the lack of warning, but I wanted to talk to you outside the office.' I'm intrigued, because she is usually calm, and I know her well enough to tell she is uncomfortable about something. She darts another glance up the street, her arms crossed.

'Come in.' I stand back to let her into the sitting room. 'Can I make you a coffee or tea?'

'A coffee would be great, thank you. White, no sugar.' I make the drinks as quickly as possible, and as she doesn't immediately start on why she's come round, we exchange inconsequential chit-chat as I do so, although I am impatient to find out what she wants.

Eventually I sit opposite her at the table, mugs steaming between us and I've even found a few biscuits to put on a plate.

'What's going on?' I know she'll appreciate the direct approach.

'Obviously it's work—' I raise my hands.

'Please don't tell me you're about to leave.' She smiles for the first time.

'I've no plans to. But the way things are, never say never.' I incline my head in complete understanding, but at least temporarily relieved.

'So, what can I help you with?'

'I hope it's more what I can help *you* with.' This conversation is becoming more intriguing by the sentence. 'I hope I'm not speaking out of turn here, but I'm not sure you're fully aware of what Rex is doing to you.'

'Well. There are a lot of things I *am* aware of.' I'm about to list them out; yelling, humiliating, undermining and belittling, disrespecting boundaries, hypocrisy. The fact he has no ability to take feedback or accept responsibility. That he frequently threatens people, particularly me, that he is a bully and that I know he is sexually harassing Trish. But then I'm reminded he is still our boss. Perhaps it isn't appropriate for me to be so open to her? At the same time, I'm keen to hear whatever it is she believes I'm not aware of. 'Why? What is it you've noticed? Or feel I need to know?' She clears her throat and wraps her elegant fingers around the mug.

'I know he's our boss, but I'm going to be frank. That's why I've come here rather than talk in the office.' I nod to encourage her, and she jumps right to it. 'He's gaslighting you.'

I stare at her blankly because, while I've heard the term, I don't fully understand what it means. 'Isn't that something peculiar to romantic relationships?' She inclines her head.

'It is, yes, and no. It can happen in any relationship. Including the one between employer and employee.'

'Oh, okay. What is it you think he's doing that's gaslighting, then? You're going to have to be specific because this is something I'm unfamiliar with.' I'm doubtful about what she could add to make me think worse of him, but I'm willing to hear her out.

'Think back a few months to when he was mad at you because you didn't go to a crucial meeting about the Gregson contract?' I don't need to think back. The whole mortifying episode rolls around my mind with alarming regularity. It was this incident which led me to start my notebook, not that it is turning out to be foolproof, either. I couldn't believe I could have forgotten anything so important for the company and for a while suspected I was losing my mind. Fiona carries on, 'I don't think you forgot about the meeting. I believe he never told you about it.'

'Why would he do that when it could have had dire consequences for the company?'

'To make you look bad. To undermine your authority.' She pauses, then brings her hands together on the table. 'Think about it. If we have any meetings booked, they go on the shared calendar. Whoever's involved, in this case you and Rex, gets a text message and email about the meeting. They get reminders. If he'd set it up properly, there's no way you wouldn't have been aware of it.'

She has a point. When I missed the meeting, I went through all my emails and messages but hadn't found anything. When I mentioned this to Rex, he told me he had no idea what I was talking about. We'd had a verbal conversation about the meeting, apparently, and I'd said I'd put it on the shared calendar. The fact it wasn't on there was therefore my fault. It was only because Rex was on the ball that he'd made the meeting at all, or so he said. I'd had no reason to doubt him and took full responsibility for the mistake. The problem was, although I was certain we had never discussed this meeting, I also had no comeback on Rex's accusation because I couldn't prove anything.

I tell Fiona all this, and she grimaces. 'That's further evidence of his gaslighting. Making you think you've forgotten something when you haven't. I know you, Alice, and you are the most organised person I know. There's no way you would have forgotten either that conversation or to put it on the calendar. His lying to you is a serious red flag.'

'Maybe. But it's not anything I can use. It would only be his word against mine.'

She rocks her head back and forth. 'Hmm, I guess you could be right with that example, but I do have something else. And this time there is proof.' I am all ears and shift forward in my seat. 'Do you remember the mistake with the VAT?' Of course I do. I've always prided myself on getting the bookkeeping right. On doing reconciliations. On filing on time, and accurately. Yet, we'd bought a second-hand company van and the entry clearly showed I'd claimed back the VAT on it, which isn't allowed. We'd therefore over-claimed the tax, which Fiona spotted at a later date and I corrected on the next return. But it smacked of incompetence. Something Rex hasn't let me forget. I couldn't work out how it happened, but it could only be because I didn't fill in the right information on our accounting software, as it was my job and something Rex has nothing to do with. Therefore, it was my responsibility and fault. This is a fact I've accepted and Rex makes me pay for, as he uses it at every opportunity to knock me further by humiliating me. Particularly if he can do so publicly.

'I don't see how Rex could have manipulated that situation. It was obviously my fault.'

'Which is what he wants you to believe. But don't forget, he has access to the accounting software, too.' She lets that sentence hang in the silence. I know he has his own login. Why, I'm not sure, because he never uses it as he doesn't know what he's doing.

'So, you're saying he logged in…' I'm being terribly slow as I try to work out what he's done.

'… and changed the entry himself.' Fiona finishes for me, in case I never get there.

'Okay…' I draw the word out to give me more thinking time, 'but again, we have no proof.'

'Ah, but we do. The audit report.'

'The audit report?' I feel I'm about to be mystified by the software yet again. But Fiona grins, terribly pleased with herself.

'Yup. It's not something many users would know about or have use for. Most of the time, there is no need to open it. But Rex's super-duper new accounting software records who made, or changed, each transaction. Or at least whose login was being used to change the entry.'

'Really?'

She nods her wise young head. 'Check the transaction on Monday.'

'Thank you.' I sit back in my chair and study her. 'Why are you doing this?' She is the one who could take my place should I leave, so it isn't in her best interests.

'You mean other than the fact I like you? There are many reasons, but I'll give you two. One, he was gossiping about you the other day – when you'd gone to get his dry-cleaning. Trying to undermine you in front of Phil and me because you'd forgotten to collect it when he'd supposedly asked you to. Not that I think he ever asked you to do that either, by the way. But we didn't like it. It's not your job anyway, and we wanted you to know we know what's going on and we'll support you in any way we can.'

I give her a big smile, and can feel a prickling pain as tears gather at the back of my eyes, because her words come as such a relief. I've felt so alone at work since Mr Marchant Senior died and to hear these words from her is overwhelming.

'Thank you, it's much appreciated. And the second reason?'

'Trish. I feel awful I haven't supported her more. You were talking to her on Friday and I realised I'd done nothing to make her feel welcome, purely because she'd attracted Rex's attention and hadn't had the gumption to tell him to do one, like I did.' I laugh.

'I didn't know he'd tried his luck with you.' Although it doesn't surprise me at all. Fiona is stylish and beautiful, and confidence oozes out of every pore. Even now, on a Sunday morning her long golden hair is up in an elegant chignon. Her well-cut clothes hang easily on her trim frame. She is a heady cocktail of attractive and it wouldn't surprise me if she and Phil didn't have a thing going on outside work. But that is the difference. If they do, they are professional and never blur the lines.

She grins. 'His faux affection didn't last long.'

'In Trish's defence, she's a fair bit younger than you and I don't think she has the tools or confidence to handle him in the way you did.'

'No, I agree. And I shouldn't have judged her for not dealing with him. I'll make it up to her, I promise. I've already started and I will bring her into the fold of the Marchant family.'

'She'll appreciate it. We should talk more in the office. Perhaps be more conspicuous in our support for each other.' She grimaces.

'I'm not sure that's a good idea. It's another reason I've come to talk to you here.'

'Why? What's going on?'

'Phil and I believe that someone has bugged the office. He thinks there are trackers on our computers anyway, but it wouldn't surprise us if there are cameras installed, too.'

I sit back in surprise. 'What makes you think that?'

'Phil has noticed times when he's been in a meeting with Rex and a client or the site manager. Rex has raised something Phil had been researching online, or had had a conversation about with one of the other project managers as an option for that particular client. But Rex mentions it specifically to make it look as though it's his idea.'

I raise my eyebrows. 'It is the sort of thing he'd do, take credit for someone else's work. That's shameful.' Then I doubt myself. 'Just suppose, though, if we were to give him the benefit of the doubt, what if Rex had actually come up with some good ideas? And they were simply similar to Phil's. Maybe he's beginning to learn something…' My words tail off when I see Fiona rolling her eyes. Her response is stern.

'They weren't similar. They were the same. Right down to the supplier lists. Phil is fuming, and you need to stop trying to see the good in that tosser.' I grimace. She is right.

'Okay, let's assume then Rex got the ideas from either listening in on conversations or watching what Phil was doing on his computer.' It is creepy. There's no doubt, and I'm stupid to not have suspected as much. But I come from a more innocent time. A time when such things were difficult to carry out. 'How has he done it? He's never come across as particularly tech savvy to me.' No more than any younger person, I suppose. But perhaps all are capable of such actions nowadays.

'Remember that weekend when, without a word of warning, he had the whole new computer system installed? We think it was then.'

'I guess it makes sense.' I shudder. The idea of Rex listening in or controlling what is going on, possibly watching videos of us, sickens me.

'I've become so paranoid I watch everything I type now, every website I go on. I didn't even warn you I was coming today by texting in case he's watching our phones, too. Although Phil doesn't think that's possible.' A horrible feeling creeps over me when I think about what Rex might have knowledge of me doing. Yes, I'd used my burner phone (although even using that term makes me feel faintly ridiculous) for the call to the police. But what if he'd heard the conversation through whatever bugging device he is using? Also, I'd called Eddie to let him know Rex was coming to the golf club and Eddie had called me back. A sick feeling churns through my stomach at what Rex might know. Although there is a glimmer of hope because I cannot believe for one second that if Rex knew I'd had a hand in him being arrested for drunk driving, he wouldn't have challenged me on it by now. He is not one for keeping his powder dry. Of course, I can't discuss any of this with Fiona, which is frustrating. But I don't want her to have any information about anything I've done that might come back to bite her in the future. If anyone is going to take the blame for bringing trouble to Rex's door, it will be me, and me alone.

She leaves soon after with an agreement for us to stay in touch, but in the meantime not to change our behaviour in the office.

The Marchant family. I'd smiled when she'd said this. I haven't thought about it for a while because recently we've been so far from the idea that originally came from Mr Marchant Senior, of course. He'd wanted everyone to like coming to work, as far as you could, and to enjoy collaborating as a team so we could all find fulfilment and pride in a job well done.

As it is, I can't remember the last time I didn't dread going to work. Rex's reign has caused me sleep issues, self-doubt and anxiety, to name but a few of the detrimental effects he has on me. But Fiona has awoken me to the truth, and while I may have been naïve regarding knowing what Rex was doing, I do have a particular set of skills at my disposal. And, far from previously thinking I'm not capable of pulling off the plan I've been considering against him, now might be exactly the right time to use them.

After Fiona leaves, I sit for a while. These revelations have produced two reactions in me. The first is relief that I'm not losing my mind. Worries which had gathered about memory issues, and which in my lowest moments I'd blown out of all proportion into being early onset dementia, have already begun to lift, easing from my mind like soft morning mist melting away under a summer sun. The second is having to contemplate how old I feel. How I didn't know any of this gaslighting stuff existed and how I've simply dismissed it as bullying. Which while still not being okay, I thought I was dealing with, or at least handling. Later in the day, I spend some time opening my eyes further by researching gaslighting online to find out for myself if this is what is going on. For hours, I disappear down one rabbit hole after another as I read all I can on the subject.

I have known something is badly wrong at work and in my relationship with Rex, but not the extent to which I am being manipulated. My research backs everything Fiona said. And more.

Gaslighting.

This puts the proper name to it.

9: A Time for Action… and Reaction

For the first time in longer than I care to remember, I can't wait to get into the office on Monday. I arrive early. Earlier even than Fiona anticipates. I switch on my computer, tapping my nails on the desk as I wait for it to warm up.

Last night I'd had to fight the urge to log in. I know it's possible to do so, but I have fought against working from home. However, it had taken all my willpower not to do so on this occasion in case Fiona is right, and the systems are being monitored. I didn't want Rex becoming suspicious about what I was doing.

I log in to the accounting software. It takes me a few moments to find the supplier I am after, but then I open the entry I made for the invoice for the van purchase.

Following what Fiona had told me to do, I open the "Audit History". And there it is. The proof of what happened.

There is a dated entry with my name against it showing I had added the invoice into the software with no VAT being claimed on it. A few days later there is a second entry called an Indirect Edit by Rex Marchant changing my original entry, so VAT was now to be claimed back. The VAT quarter had then ended, and the Return submitted.

Thinking back, it was odd Rex had raised the issue at the time because once we'd submitted the Return, he'd claimed that he believed, "there was something a bit off with the amount of VAT we were paying". I'd forgotten that link in the sequence of events when Fiona was with me yesterday. He'd asked Fiona to check the entries, and the error had come to light. Naturally, he'd not had a quiet word with me about the matter, but broadcast it across the office, only adding to my humiliation. It's my job to enter the purchase invoices, so there was no question it was my fault. Or so he'd led me to believe. I've certainly taken full responsibility for it.

In the Audit Log, there was a third entry recorded, this time in my name, showing I'd corrected the error. A smile spreads across my face and as Fiona arrives and removes her jacket, she catches my eye, a knowing look passing between us.

I can't believe I actually have some proof to back Fiona's accusation of Rex gaslighting me and am incredibly relieved to find I wasn't at fault. I've lost a lot of confidence over the issue and had started to believe I am at best incompetent and at worst going mad, so finding this proof means a huge weight lifts from my shoulders. At the same time, anger flares right in the centre of my being. The more I ponder what he's done, the bigger the flame grows. Rex gave me considerable grief for this "mistake". His voice had been loud enough to make sure everyone could hear when he'd told me my work was slapdash and that I was "clearly incapable" of doing even the most basic of tasks, when all along he'd sabotaged my work. Unforgivable. That's what it is.

I wonder why he's gaslit me. I thought he'd value me when he took over but he's only ever wanted me gone and this is how he's chosen to go about it. My anger won't let me dwell for long on fathoming his reasons, though. I haven't the patience for it but I'm certainly not about to let him get away with it.

Rex usually has nothing to do with the bookkeeping or the accounting software and, as far as I'm aware, he knows little about how it works, but he has proven he knows enough. I am sure, though, he won't be aware of the software recording each user's transactions. I'm therefore confident he won't know there is such a thing as an Audit Report. Even if he finds out about it, he can't tamper with it, so there is no danger of him being able to delete it.

Rex has made a major error. He has proven himself to be an amateur in trying to mess with me. Because he hasn't a clue who he is dealing with.

But he will. I'll make sure of it.

Enough indecision. I could challenge him on his gaslighting now I have proof. But only being able to do so on the one instance of it feels unsatisfactory.

Instead, I choose to use this discovery as my motivation to take action.

Because I have a plan that will bring him down.

And there will be no mistakes.

I fume at my desk for a few hours before Rex arrives at a tardy eleven o'clock. I am pleased to see he ignores Trish. Better he be thought rude than lecherous.

He walks past my office door and fails to respond to my, 'Good morning.'

An hour later, he reappears. 'I'll be off at three, so if there's anything you need from me, you'd best get it done by then.'

'Off where?'

'None of your business. I'll be back after the bank holiday.'

Although one part of me thinks, *are you kidding me?* The bigger part cheers, *hurrah! An entire week without him.* However, taken aback, I can't help my response. 'You're away until next Tuesday? Why is this the first I've heard of yet another holiday?'

He takes a step closer to my desk. 'I did tell you. Clearly, it's something else you've forgotten. But it hardly matters anyway as it's only a short week with it being Easter.' The liar didn't tell me, and we may have a four-day weekend coming up, but that's hardly the point.

'Rex, you're meant to be running this company. The least you could do is tell me if you're not going to be here. Or put it on the calendar.'

He scowls. I know I'm trying his patience, but as I'm at the end of my tether with him, he's also trying mine. 'I've already said I did tell you. It's not my fault you're so incompetent, you can't remember. It's your job to manage the calendar, not mine. Besides, I don't see why I need to tell you anything as it all runs itself, anyway.' There is no point in arguing over who told whom what, so I move on because, following the proof of his gaslighting earlier, this might be just the opportunity I can use to my advantage. I ignore the fleeting tremor of panic that runs through me at the mere thought of what I'm about to do.

'It doesn't run itself, and there might be things I need you to sign off on?'

'Like?'

'I won't know until they actually happen, will I. And you've given me no time to plan and prepare for progressing everything else.' My thoughts scatter as I try to work out what I will need from him as I continue, 'There are contracts for you to sign before you go and I haven't even drafted them yet.'

'Then I suggest you get on with it.' He taps his watch. 'Time's ticking.' *God, he's irritating.*

As I scrabble around for the files, I say, 'But what about anything else we might need you for? This is too short notice, Rex.'

'You know my number, so call me, although my phone will probably be off. Not much of a holiday if it's on, is it?' One hand is on the edge of the door where he taps his finger, then glances back. 'Or you could just make the decisions yourself. You usually do anyway, seeing as this godawful place is the most exciting part of what passes for your sad little life.' As he intended, his words sting, but I don't respond, not even when his eyebrows lift in expectation. After what I've discovered this morning, I don't know what might come out should I open my mouth. Not only do I not want to give anything away, but my retaliation will exacerbate the situation. So, with nothing forthcoming, he gives a slight shake of his head. Which I take as irritation or perhaps disappointment that I haven't risen to the bait, and he walks off. I relax my jaw, which I had to clench to keep back the words I wanted to hurl at him. Because that wouldn't do. That wouldn't do at all.

I reflect on all the things I read yesterday about how to respond to an abusive boss. Tackling him head-on is not one of the approved methods.

I need to be stealthy in my approach, if indeed I am going to approach at all, because I'm already second-guessing my decision to take action.

Even though I'm short of time to get everything in place for his departure, I need a few minutes and go to make myself a cup of tea. I attempt to calm myself as I dunk the tea bag in and out of the water repeatedly, thinking about the things he said. One phrase keeps repeating in my mind and, as I return to my desk and draft the contracts, I contemplate whether it is possible to carry on if things stay as they are because this working situation is intolerable. Fortunately, I am adept at putting contracts together. I've been doing them for so long, so as I draft I continue to consider the situation, and my way forward. If there even is a way forward because I seriously question whether I can continue to work for this obnoxious man if everything remains the same. I know what I *should* do. I should simply walk away and get a job elsewhere. That would be the sensible choice. But something, a ferociously tenacious something deep in the core of my soul, can't allow me to do it.

Or you could just make the decisions yourself.

That's what he'd said. That is the phrase I can't get out of my head.

Hmm. It has a nice ring to it.

And it aligns so perfectly with my plans.

Can I successfully engineer such an outcome? And do I want to? Wouldn't it be better for me to take what I can and run? That is an easier solution to the problem.

Either way I will be taking control of my own fate, and that feels better than leaving it in the hands of others.

Thoughts like these have been running through my mind for a while now and, at various low points, I've made some arrangements. Mostly to make me feel better, or at least make me feel I've got a back-up plan. Or the start of one. But I hadn't expected to be putting my half-prepared plans into action this quickly, or even at all. I know I've been going over them at home but, in reality, will they even work?

My hand is being forced, though, because of Rex's imminent departure. I contemplate leaving it until another time, a time when perhaps I'll be more prepared but with all I've found out recently, something in me, and I daresay something of the spirit of George, comes alive and tells me to react and seize the day.

Decided, my heartbeat quickens as the list of all I have to do grows rapidly. Timing is everything, as is carrying out what I need to in the right order. For me to achieve anything though, as before when I've been laying the foundations for my plan, I need Rex to be on site but out of his office for as long as possible.

I gaze over at Fiona and Phil, both hard at work, and my spirits sink. What I am about to set in motion will change everything, and while my plan is to save everyone's jobs and the company from further ruin, if unsuccessful, I could potentially be putting their livelihoods at risk. While such an outcome no longer bothers me for my own sake, what about them? Will the gains be worth taking the chance? I remind myself he'd called his father's pride and joy a "godawful place" and my hackles rise. I deliberate on this for a short while. Some might call it dithering, but eventually I make my decision. After all, I have been through the plans in detail at home and there I was certain I could achieve what I wanted to and only implicate myself and not the others.

If I do nothing, we might lose the company and everyone's jobs, anyway. There is always that.

I walk over to Phil Baxter's desk. 'Phil, Rex has told me he's going to be away for the next week. I think you said there was a project issue you wanted to run past him? Something to do with the plans for the Foreman job? If it's still the case, you'd better check in with him before he goes at three.'

Phil's expression is blank for mere seconds before he catches on and nods enthusiastically. 'Ahh, yes. Thanks for letting me know. I do need to speak to him.'

'I would imagine it would be best to lay out those plans in The Lodge, wouldn't it?' I continue as he reaches into the bottom drawer of his desk and draws out a file.

'Yes. We'll need the space. I'll see if Eddie's around, then I can bring Rex in to discuss the scheduling of the project and all the, er, plans.'

'Perfect. I assume it will take a while, so as soon as you're ready?' Again, he nods as though in full understanding and I turn to include Fiona in the conversation. 'With Rex about to take a week's leave, could you both check through anything else you might need to speak to him about today, please?' This is what should be considered as due process with any imminent staff absence, and while we'll go through the motions, it is laughable as far as Rex is concerned as he contributes nothing, does even less, and in reality, we don't need him for any of the day-to-day decision making. Although his signature is required on anything official. That is one of a few things he insists upon to make it appear as though he is in charge.

I go back to my office and download recent bank transactions into the accounting software. As adrenaline courses through my body, my muscles become twitchy and my thoughts difficult to keep focused on any one task. I'm pleased to see the first fifty thousand pounds has come in from Tony Scampton. Right on time.

Rex sticks his head round his office door. 'Have you got those contracts done yet?'

'Nearly,' I reply. 'I'm getting together a pile of things which need your signature, then I'll be in so we can get it done in one go instead of in dribs and drabs.' That's just the sort of helpful person I am.

He checks his watch. 'Make it quick. Phil needs me to meet with him shortly.'

I finish the contracts and stack the necessary paperwork together, hating what I have to do next, but I gather every ounce of courage I have, pick up the pile on my desk and with a quick knock on his door, enter his office. I could pass out at any moment, my breaths are that light, my feet unsteady on his deep pile carpet.

'You took your time.'

I nearly bite back, but manage to hold it in. 'There was a lot to prepare.' The next few minutes are crucial, and my hands shake as I place the pile on his desk. While he doesn't appreciate any of it, I aim everything at making his life easier, so I've placed coloured tags on each document to indicate every place he has to sign. I take a deep breath as he withdraws his fountain pen – he likes his sprawling signature to have flourish – and I pray he doesn't ask questions.

Rex peers at the first contract, checks the name it is in, and, satisfied, signs, then slides the papers to one side to get to the next. My heart jumps with this action. I can't afford for him to do that, and it is out of character. He scans over the next document too, but then, happy or perhaps already bored, he reverts to type, merely lifting the corner of the pile of papers in front of him to get to the next tag before signing where I'd indicated. Then, repeating this process through the entire pile, he signs each of the following papers in quick succession. He only pauses once. Blue print on white. The bank.

'What's this?' My heart leaps so far up my throat it's a surprise I can get any words out.

'It's the change to the mandate you wanted. To add Fiona on to the online banking.' My lies flow like ripples in a stream.

'Okay. An excellent decision of mine.' I imagine him thinking it is one more step along the path to me no longer being needed.

There is only one more sticky patch when he pauses and, for one horrible moment, it appears as though he is going to pull the document he has just signed out of the pile to examine it further. I think I might faint, I've held my breath for so long, but then it is over. Everything is back in my hands and signed. I hold the pile of paperwork clutched to my chest as though my life depends on it as I exit his office.

Before I'd gone in to see Rex, I'd noticed Phil had spent a few minutes checking the Foreman project file after I'd spoken to him. Then he made a call, I presumed to see where Eddie was. When I walk back out, he checks his watch, then reaches for his jacket hung on the back of his chair and shrugs it on, before taking the file and heading towards Rex's office. If he feels the same level of trepidation as I do on entering, he doesn't show it, because you never know which Rex you are about to encounter. The calm version, who will at least attempt to play a part in the running of this company, or the one who will bawl you out for merely glancing in his direction. At least today the pre-holiday Rex is in an accommodating mood, and a few minutes later, he follows Phil out of the building and across the yard.

I peer from the window, and as soon as they've disappeared into The Lodge I go into Rex's office, pleased to see his computer is on. I quickly log in to the security cameras and make some necessary adjustments. It is time to get down to business. Yet at this crucial moment, my courage deserts me. I know what I need to do. I know I have limited time in which to do it. But once in front of the computer I sit, staring at the screen, unsure whether I am doing the right thing. Is this the best time? I ask myself. It isn't as if I haven't already given the problem a lot of consideration and put effort into the planning, but I hadn't expected to be making this move today so I feel unprepared and as though I am going off half-cocked. I don't like it. It makes me unsettled. What if, by rushing into this, I can't ultimately pull it off and get myself out of the predicament I find myself in with Rex? Once I make my move, there is no going back.

The other side of my mind argues that with Rex about to go on holiday for a week, it is too good an opportunity to miss. As I toy with these thoughts back and forth, it becomes obvious it's far easier to do nothing. I could go back to my desk. Cover, as usual, for Rex and carry on being the one who runs the company but gets precious little for it. But the resentment that has built over the years has reached a level which makes me baulk at that idea. Why should I continue to put up with it? Why shouldn't I take what is mine? And why didn't Mr Marchant Senior leave me the shares he'd assured me he would? Then none of this would be necessary.

I hear George's voice again. His encouragement. "If not now, then when", his favourite phrase repeats on a loop. "When" may never come. So, heart in mouth, I make my decision. Enough is enough. I sign in to the bank, do what I have to do, and log back out. I have documents to scan and a couple of other sites to work through, too, and I curse myself for wasting time dithering about earlier when I need every moment. While I carry out all the tasks on the checklist in my head, I bob in the office chair like a manic jack-in-the-box, peeping out of the window to check there is no sign of Rex on his way back. All the while, my heart flutters against my ribs like a trapped bird because while I've had some of these actions planned for a while, I'd imagined I'd have more time to see them through. That I wouldn't have been rushed into this step. This important step, the one I need to take my time over. The action step. When rushing can so easily cause a mistake, a misstep. And I can't afford a single one. Panicking, as time is surely running out, I deal with the relentless series of emails which pop into Rex's inbox in response to my actions, cursing the level of checks and double-checks all organisations carry out nowadays and remembering back to the days before we all went digital when this was so much easier, and shaking my head at the situation I am in. At the situation I've put myself in. It's ludicrous. How the hell did I ever think this was going to work? There are so many things that can go wrong. So many ways something might tip him off to what I have done. If I'm discovered he will throw me out immediately. He'll have every right. There'll be no reference, and I'll never get another job. I feel sick at the glee my sacking will bring him. If I fail, I will give him all he needs to get rid of me and probably have me arrested. There will be no reprieve.

Failure is therefore not an option.

I glance out of the window again and there he is leaving The Lodge; Phil is talking earnestly to him as though to keep his attention and slow the pace. I have seconds before he enters this building and I can't explain myself if he catches me coming out of his office. I rapidly close tabs and put everything back as it should be and where it belongs in his drawer. A final check of his inbox reassures me there is nothing incriminating in there and, heart pounding, I walk swiftly to my office, barely making it back behind my desk before he is in reception and coming my way. Pretending to be working away like the diligent little soul I am, I try to relax my shoulders and calm my breathing.

It is done, and there is no going back. I might have done what is right, but nausea claws at my stomach like a rabid beast.

As Rex disappears into his office, every nerve is on high alert. Every sinew taut with tension. My heart pounds as I expect him to have received something, some notification or email, something I've overlooked which will alert him to my actions. In my mind, I imagine him storming back out, his accusations brutal. I jump at a noise outside, thinking it's his office door, my hand flying to my chest in fright as I take some deep breaths to steady myself. As the minutes pass, as the immediate danger is over, I feel calmer. But time can't pass quickly enough now, each second dragging to the next, because the sooner he is out of the office, the better.

I exchange a nod of thanks with Phil when I catch his eye, then Fiona comes over to my office.

'Everything all right?' she says, no doubt mystified by my actions. I'm not going to share any details with her, either here or outside the office, as it is best she, and everyone else here know nothing. At least then I'm only jeopardising my own job.

'Yes, fine. Here are the signed contracts,' and I pick them out of the pile and hand them over. 'Can you progress them, please?'

'Of course. Anything else you need doing?'

'No, I think that's it for the moment, thank you,' I say, and give her as steady a smile as I can manage. I then place the rest of the paperwork in my desk drawer. It can wait until Rex has left.

The time spent at my desk from then on is interminable. The threat of discovery remains in every second and I can't wait for him to leave for his holiday. So sure am I that at any moment Rex will launch himself out of his office in a rage that I can't concentrate on anything. In an attempt to distract myself, I deal with a couple of simple email responses but in reality do little but stare at the screen and let the minutes creep past, my pulse pounding in my ears as I count each lethargic second.

The tension ratcheted in my body is so tight that, although I expect it, I still jump when his office door does eventually open. But with everything to lose, I play my part and manage to maintain my focus on my screen, only acknowledging him as he stops by my door. I hold my breath. He says not one word about anything to do with the business over the coming week, but I know he will have switched over all responsibility to me. That knowledge, which sweeps like a wave of relief through every molecule of my body, releases a good deal of the stress I carry.

'I'm off now.'

'Have a good time.'

That is the extent of our conversation before he walks out of the office without another word to anyone else. My part is said out of duty rather than any wish he would in fact have a good time. I don't even know where he is going. But I do know he'll have diverted his incoming emails from now on to my inbox. That is what I've been waiting for. The threat of him being tipped off from now on considerably less likely.

Although many people with any level of responsibility still read, and reply to, necessary emails while they are on leave these days, he doesn't. That is not a holiday he has told me, often, because he is away frequently. He has a point, but in his role it is remiss of him not to at least read them. This lax attitude of his works in my favour, though, because from now on, it is my job. I also curate what he has waiting for him on his return.

My computer pings as a few emails arrive in my inbox and sure enough some for Rex are among them. Curiously, one appears to be a response I sent to a supplier only a few minutes ago. Odd. I don't remember copying Rex into the email. There is no reason I would have done. I open my sent items to check and no, I didn't copy him in. I sit back in my chair to think. As I'm not technologically minded, I'm not sure how this could have happened. I glance over at Phil. He's good with computers. I could ask him, but then something Fiona said on Sunday comes to mind.

"Phil and I believe that someone has bugged the office. He thinks there are trackers on our computers anyway, but it wouldn't surprise us if there are cameras installed, too".

Is Rex keeping an eye on my emails? Is it even possible? If it is, it must be something he can turn off and on, as otherwise I'd have noticed during his previous absences. I sit for a few minutes trying to think through how it might work. I must have sent the email to the supplier then Rex had switched off his access to my emails and diverted his inbox to me before he'd refreshed it, allowing this one to come in later, to me. Because of Fiona's warning, I can't speak to Phil now, but I need to check this with him at some point. For the time being, I save the email in a folder I use for random things I think I might need as proof of Rex's behaviour, should it ever be required.

I'm an organised person, in case you haven't already noticed, and as such I keep up to date with my everyday tasks. Now I have put things in motion. I go through the next week in my diary to see if there is anything important to deal with. There is nothing out of the ordinary as far as I can see. I drink a cup of tea, contemplating a little longer then, as is usual practice for me, I go round to each member of staff, all busy at their desks, to see what they are doing, whether there are any issues and if they are on top of their tasks. Everything is running smoothly.

I also pop over to The Lodge. It's late afternoon by now, so the builder's vans are returning. Their occupants start work before the office staff, so finish earlier too. I smile cheerfully at those present and receive plenty of smiles in return. Here, at least, most are unaware of the pressure I am under in the office. Rex's manner has also not affected the employees to the same degree as inside, so it is a more relaxing part of the company to be in. Most of the workers are keen to leave their work vehicles and clock out for the day, so don't hang around. A few of the more senior staff are chatting in the large meeting room. Not as well appointed as the administration building, it is practical with concrete floors which are easier to clean considering those who use it have largely come off building sites in all weathers, and so it is perfect for the role it plays. The room is dominated by a large table which has plans spread across it. There is plenty of seating to enable all to sit comfortably to go through planning sessions and of course there are drinks machines which Mr Marchant Senior and I ensured dispense decent coffee and tea. At least those standards haven't dropped, as I glance round the room to make sure everything is in order.

Eddie Lumbers enters, his hard hat under his arm. 'I hear the big boss man has disappeared again for a week.' He smiles, which I can't help but reciprocate, but then it crosses my mind Rex might have bugged or be watching this building too. Perhaps when I have the opportunity away from here, I should mention this to Eddie. I'd hate for anyone to get into trouble for saying something they shouldn't.

'Yes, he's gone. It's been a bit of a rush getting everything organised before he left.'

'I can imagine. You probably need the trip he's going on more than he does.' He piques my curiosity.

'Do you know where he's going?'

'Yes, don't you?'

'No, I didn't want to give him the satisfaction of asking.' He chuckles. I hold my hands up. 'I know, I'm too stubborn for my own good.'

'He's off for a week at a spa in some fancy hotel in Scotland.'

'Sounds delightful. You're right, I could do with a relaxing week at a spa.' I walk over to the coffee machine to check on supplies. 'Is everything all right over here?'

'Yes, we have work scheduled in for the next few weeks. And we have a long weekend to look forward to. Do you have any plans for it?'

'Not particularly. Other than having a break.'

'Me too. Although I need to come and make up those vegetable beds for you at some point. Do you think it's something we could make a start on?'

'Oh, yes. That would be great. Don't put yourself out, though. If you have other plans, another week or so won't make any difference.'

'I shall check my social calendar and see if I can fit it in,' he says with a smile, and I suspect his is probably about as busy as mine. As I check the stock of tea and coffee, he finishes with, 'I'll call you and we'll sort out timings,' then we go our separate ways.

Despite all the difficulties Rex creates in the business and with the staff, they are a solid bunch right now, which I am thankful for, considering morale is at rock bottom. It is noticeable how the atmosphere lifts whenever Rex walks away from the admin building. It is the same in The Lodge. I've imagined it is only me who notices the difference in his absence but no, gentle banter starts around me again whenever he leaves The Lodge after a meeting, and if I remain to chat with staff, it is noticeable. Maybe I shouldn't get so uptight when he goes on one of his holidays, and perhaps encourage his absences instead.

It's a shame because I know if he'd shown any interest as a child, his father would have been delighted to have him around more and would have guided him through the ins and outs of the business. If that had happened, Rex wouldn't have felt thrown into the deep end when disaster struck, and perhaps we would not be in the situation we are now in.

It is this my mind dwells upon as I go back to my office. I open up a new document on my computer and begin typing some notes.

Once five-thirty comes, the other employees begin to leave, and we say our goodbyes. Trish is the last to go and pokes her head in through my door as she pulls her coat on.

'Are you working late again?'

I pull my focus away from my screen, keen to sow some seeds. 'I shouldn't be too long. I have some things to finish so I need to get those done, then I'll be off as I'm not feeling great.'

'Sorry to hear that. I hope you're not coming down with something.'

'Same here. Actually, seeing as it's just us, I wanted to see how everything had been since I had a chat with Rex.'

'Ah, a chat, you call it,' and she raises her eyebrows. 'It's been great actually, as he completely ignores me unless he has to ask me for something directly.'

'Excellent. Are you feeling all right about it?'

'I am, and I'm relieved. I hadn't realised how worried I'd been.'

'That's good to hear, but I hope he doesn't continue with the frosty treatment for too long. It could be equally wearing.'

'Hopefully he'll come back in a better mood after his holiday.'

'Fingers crossed. Have a safe journey home, Trish.'

She smiles as she waves goodbye. 'You too, and don't work too late.'

She's a sweet girl and sounds as if she cares. It will be nice if I can manage to protect her from Rex's clutches long term, but I'm not sure if my plans will ensure that or not yet.

I work on my document for the next hour, keen not to leave anything out. If my scheming results in me not returning, at least there will be this. Once satisfied, I pin the file to my desktop, leaving it prominent so anyone signing in can find it.

Next, I take a quick tour of the offices to make sure everything is in order. I finish in Rex's office, tiding his desk and putting away some client files he'd left out. Whilst they aren't exactly confidential, the company should be as discreet as possible in all matters pertaining to clients and, as the cleaners will be arriving later, temptation shouldn't be in their path. I fill a tray with the mugs and plates Rex has abandoned, including a couple of glasses that, from the smell of them, had contained whisky, carrying it into the kitchenette for washing.

Finally I clear my desk, leaving it as I would want to find it and do my checks through my files. I am about to lock up and turn out the lights when the cleaners arrive. We use a small local company led by the formidable Maureen. I haven't seen her in months, as they usually arrive much later in the evening.

'I 'ope it's all right us turnin' up early,' she says, and adjusts her tabard as she gets out of her van, accompanied by her husband, Dennis.

'Of course. It's good to see you. Are you both well?'

'Yeah, not much to grumble about. Still, that don't stop 'im,' she laughs. Thankfully, her husband is smiling, and it probably isn't the first time he's heard it. 'We won't 'old you up because we need to get done as we're off out tonight.'

'Super, for anything special?'

'Our wedding anniversary. Forty years. Can you believe it?'

Dennis chips in, 'I told 'er I'd 'ave got less for murder.' Then chuckles to himself as I join in. I imagine there have been many times he's laughed at that particular joke over the years.

'Congratulations! Have a great evening.' It's a shame I didn't know beforehand as I'd have sent them a gift. But I can do it tomorrow. I am about to leave then remember something and turn back. 'Oh, and thank you for the new air fresheners you've put in, they've got a lovely fresh citrus scent.'

There is some distance between us now and Maureen says, 'Oh, that were nothing to do with us. Mr Marchant deals with those.'

'Oh? Has he always done that?' It seems most unlike him.

'Yeah, we came in one night a few years back an' 'e was still 'ere. It was when the computers were being changed over. 'e told us 'e was putting 'em in then and this lot are the replacements. We 'ad noticed them.'

'Okay.' Taken aback, I have nothing more to say on the subject so continue on towards my car, still amazed by the fact Rex has been in the office late at night for something that didn't involve drinking with his friends. Although, I suppose, perhaps it still did. Anyway, wonders will never cease. As with the computer system, he has surprised me again. It's a shame, though, that the bits he does decide to do for the company are so random.

I ignore the niggle this exchange causes deep in the back of my mind as I have far too much going on to dwell any longer on office cleaning, and I return to the matter in hand which is already giving me much to fret about. Now I've walked out, a flutter accelerates in my chest, my throat, as I cross the car park to where my car stands all alone, my heartbeat rising at what I've done as I get in. I gaze at the building where I've spent the majority of my working life, and tears well up as this could be the end. Will I be back or will I be discovered? That is the big question. While I believe I have done everything necessary to cover my tracks, what I can't account for is the degree to which Rex is spying on me via the computer. It won't take a lot for him to put two and two together and conclude I am to blame for all his misfortune.

However, I am a decent judge of character and I know his. When it comes to it, the truth is, and I am betting my future and dare I say it the future of Marchant & Son on it, that Rex is inherently lazy, and an idiot. If he is spying on us, I am certain the first wave of excitement that produced has long since worn off. While he may have diligently pored over all the information he received initially, I doubt he has the work ethic to still be checking anything regularly. As I reverse out of my space then drive away, I cannot refuse myself one last glance in the rear-view mirror, hoping I am not about to be proven wrong.

10: The Six Ps

Proper Planning Prevents Piss-Poor Performance. I heard that once and it applies to the situation I find myself in. Only I'm agitated I've not done the proper planning. Today didn't exactly go as expected. Rushed into acting, I spend the evening filled with second thoughts I've proceeded too hastily. Perhaps I can go back to the office tomorrow and undo what I've done, pretend it never happened and carry on as normal. But even as I contemplate this option, I know I can't go back. Not only has everything changed since Mr Marchant Senior died, and the job I'd once loved has gone, but there is the small matter of the first fifty thousand pounds I've already transferred. Even if I cancel the follow-up payments, there is no explaining what happened with that one. No, there is no option. If it comes to it, it is time to make my move. I'd never expected to be there for so long anyway. The job was only meant to have been a stopgap to keep a roof over my head while I worked out what to do next. Instead, it has become the major part of my life. After Rex took over, it isn't as if I hadn't known I would leave one day. That has become clear, but I'd not expected that "one day" to possibly be today.

I imagine George's reaction had I come home and told him the news that I might have just walked out of my job. Then I smile to myself. Delighted. That's what he'd have been and he'd have told me it was about time.

'Come on, old girl. On to the next adventure,' he would have said. Another of his favourite sayings. If I'm being honest with myself, I'd considered my days for adventure over, despite all my recent planning. In reality, if Mr Marchant Senior were alive, I'd never have done what I did today. I would have had no need; I would have been happy to have continued working there forever. But Rex has pushed and pushed and pushed, and today I've jumped.

What exactly will my next adventure be? While I'm not sure if what I've put in motion today will work out, I feel a twist of nausea at the possibility of leaving my settled life and striking out into something new.

No need to rush, though. No need to run tonight. I have a few days' grace before my absence will cause alarm bells to ring. With Rex away, longer before anyone spots the missing money. I've made sure of it.

The thing is, despite how he talks to me and treats me, Rex trusts me. He must do because he insists I deal with all the online banking transactions, despite him having the ability to do them himself. At my most paranoid, I've assumed it is because if there are any errors, he can plant them firmly at my door. When in a more optimistic mood, I know it makes sense for one person to take overall charge and responsibility for such matters. Mostly, I suppose it is yet another example of his lazy nature, it being one less thing for him to have to do. Oh, yes, one thing is certain in our relationship, despite everything he trusts me. What a fool he is.

It doesn't mean he doesn't keep an eye on the bank account, though. It will be the first thing he will check on his return. I've noticed his pattern because I always get a deluge of questions about various transactions which have happened in his absence.

The only other thing Rex is territorial about is his post. Considering everything else I do for him, he still thinks the fact he doesn't allow me to open and handle anything addressed to him shows he is in charge. I am fine with that. It is one less thing for me to manage and no hardship to deliver anything addressed to him to the tray on his desk. The only problem is he never gets round to opening it. The stack gets ever higher until we are missing something vital (most recently it was his new passport) and it is only when I carefully suggest to him it might be in the pile on his desk that he gives in and gets me to open it all. Which surely misses the point he was presumably trying to make in the first place? When I mentioned this once, I was told to shut up.

I've often pondered why he is so possessive about the post, and if he is involved in something he shouldn't be. Despite scrutinising the envelopes he's received, I haven't seen anything that appears to be out of the ordinary with any of them. I've therefore simply explained it away as one of his idiosyncrasies.

A spear of alarm shoots through me. What if the bank contacts him? Questions the fact that fifty thousand pounds is due to leave the business account every day for the next few days?

'Don't worry about what you can't control.' George's familiar voice in my ear causes me to let out my breath with relief. He's right. I can do nothing about it now and, anyway, it isn't as if the bank isn't used to large sums of money going into and out of the account. Why would it raise any alert with them? I am panicking and finding issues where there are none.

What to do next? That is what I should be concentrating on.

My preferred option right now is to run away. I go to my bedroom, pull out my passport from its hiding place at the back of my knicker drawer, and open it. Bugger. My stomach drops.

It has expired. That's what happens when you're rushed into taking action before you've finished thinking everything through. I sit on the edge of my bed and consider the way forward. It isn't as if I haven't had recent experience of renewing a passport. I did it only weeks ago for Rex and know I don't have the time to wait around for it to be posted, processed and posted back. However appealing an idea, it appears fleeing the country is no longer a possibility and instead I will have to face the music once my actions catch up with me. Although I then consider if things go in a certain way, this failure to have a valid passport in place could work in my favour and bolster my position. In order for that to happen, though, I need to ensure events unfold in the way I intend them to, and I only have this week to work them through and make sure there are no pitfalls.

11: Ham and Pineapple

On Tuesday morning I call Fiona as soon as the office opens, full of snuffles, my voice as croaky as I can manage.

'I'm sorry to do this to you, but I think I have the flu and I don't think I can make it in.' I hate lying to her, but needs must.

'Poor you. I hope you're taking care of yourself?'

'I ache all over and can't keep anything down, so I'm in bed. It isn't ideal with Rex away, but do you think between you, you can hold the fort? I'm not sure when I'm going to get back in.'

'Of course we can.'

'If you could keep on top of the bookkeeping, it would be helpful.'

'I'll do what I can, but the bank transactions aren't coming in.' I know they wouldn't be as I switched off the updates yesterday. Only Rex or I can re-authorise the connection. It is what I've had to do to ensure the sight of all those thousands leaving the account doesn't alarm her.

'Bother. I didn't realise they were due for reauthorisation. Do what you can and we'll get the rest sorted out once I'm back.'

'No problem. I'll let everyone know what's happened, and you rest. It's a short week here, anyway.'

'I'm only a phone call away if you need me. And I don't think there's any need to tell Rex. I'd send him a message, but it's not as though he's going to cancel his holiday to come back and help, is it?'

She laughs. 'No, he won't. We'll be fine, don't worry. You need to concentrate on getting better. Oh, and so you know,

Trish and I are going out together for a quick lunch today. Phil and the others have said they'll handle the phones while we're gone.'

'That's great, thanks.' I end the call feeling better about those I've left behind.

My next call is to a local florist, where I put in an order for a large bouquet, in shades of ruby red, and a box of chocolates to be sent to Maureen and Dennis.

I then look around my cottage and contemplate doing all the things I never have time for. The fact I can't go out and about hampers me, but I have last week's shopping in the fridge that I've done nothing with and a freezer full of ingredients that need to be made into something. After a period of organisation and recipe research, I spend the rest of the day cooking and baking to fill the freezer and fridge with meals and goodies to last me for weeks.

Exhausted but satisfied with all I've produced, by the evening I'm content to curl up on the sofa and watch the television for a few hours.

The next morning, I clear out the spare bedroom so I can freshen it with a coat of paint. I've always been envious of how beautiful Dora has made her cottage and I've been meaning to do better in mine for years, but although I bought the paint and the materials I need months ago, I've not got around to it. When I've asked some decorators at work for tips, preparation is the most important part of the process, so I prepare the surfaces and woodwork as best I can.

Mid-morning, I go downstairs for a coffee and a sizeable piece of cake after my efforts and notice the post has arrived. In amongst the junk mail is an addressed envelope: fountain pen, card-sized, quality. My interest is piqued as it's so rare to receive anything personal nowadays. It contains an invitation to what is surely going to be the wedding of the century, at least in these parts. Jocasta, the only daughter of Barry and Cordelia Jones (although I note she's used *her* hyphenated Hampton-Jones on the invitation) is getting married in June to a Nicholas Salisbury. How exciting and unexpected. Who else will I know there and how did I get an invitation in the first place? It can only be because both Barry and I are in M.A.T.S (Melton Amateur Theatrical Society) because Cordelia's and my life don't intersect at any point.

After the ceremony in the church, the reception is to be held at The Grange, the Joneses' place and the largest property in the village. Its drive is so long one can barely see the property from the road, and no one I know is a regular visitor. I've also heard Barry and Cordelia have had the entire garden landscaped and now I'm going to get the chance to see it for myself. I'll have to get a new outfit, of course, and I mull this over while I finish my cake and coffee.

My spare room is small, so I get two coats on the ceiling by the evening. I may not be a professional, or even an enthusiastic amateur, but I've made a decent stab at it and my efforts please me.

Eddie calls me in the evening. I only remember I am meant to be ill as I answer, but sound feeble enough in time.

'Are you okay? I heard you had the flu.'

'Yes, I'm feeling grotty.'

'You must be to not come into work. That's unheard of.' I know he's teasing me. I do take time off, although now I come to think of it, I can't remember the last time I was off ill.

'Haha. I'm as prone to sickness as everyone else. It's best not to come in and spread it about. I've only just been able to get out of bed.'

'Have you eaten anything?'

'Only some dry biscuits. I can't face anything else.'

'Can I do some shopping for you? Is there anything you think you might be able to eat? Or do you need any medication?'

'It's kind of you, but I've got all I need here.'

'Even brandy?' I smile, as it is his go-to cure for everything, he has told me as much before.

'Even brandy.' I pause, appreciating his kindness. He appears so keen to help and genuinely disappointed I don't need him, so I try to make him feel better. 'If I think of anything, I'll call, okay?'

'That'll be grand. I've also got the sleepers you wanted for the raised beds. If you're well enough, I could make a start at the weekend. It turns out my social calendar had nothing pressing on it.' He makes me smile again.

'I'm sure I'll be better by then. Certainly not infectious, which is the main thing.'

'There you are, always thinking of everyone else.' I'm not sure how to respond and there's a longer than feels comfortable silence before he finishes with, 'Feel better soon, Alice. And call me if you need anything, particularly if you run out of brandy.'

We didn't speak one word about work during the conversation. Which must be a first. It was good of him to call. I've had a couple of text messages from Fiona checking in on me, but otherwise I've been in touch with no one.

I wake early the following morning and set about painting the walls a lovely fresh forget-me-not blue. One coat by breakfast, the other after.

Guilty about not making my usual site visit in the afternoon, I call the site office. I need not have worried as Fiona has already alerted them to my absence and everything is in hand. No one is indispensable.

Desperate for some fresh air, I walk up the garden in the afternoon. I enjoy gardening and want to grow some vegetables. Although other than mentioning it in passing to Eddie one day, a while ago now, I've done nothing more about it. Clearly he hasn't forgotten and has been considerably more proactive than me in progressing the project, which is a surprise. If I want to grow anything this year, I know I'd better get on with it so his making a start on the build at the weekend will be helpful. As I'm mulling over my vegetable plans and thinking I'd better research some planting ideas, I spot Dora over the wall, coming towards me. She's wearing a beaming smile as she strides out.

'You will never guess what has happened?'

'What? Are you okay?'

'Better than okay. She has called.' I have an idea who, but this is such fragile ground I don't want to guess.

'Who's called?'

'Rosie. My daughter! Well, she's not Rosie now, of course. They called her Esme. But it's fine, isn't it? It is a beautiful name.' I reach over the wall between us and clasp her hands.

'It is a beautiful name.' She is fizzing with joy, and it's infectious. I'm laughing and crying with her as she tells me every detail of the call. Apparently, Esme has been trying to get in touch since Mother's Day. She hadn't wanted to leave a message, and finally they'd spoken. For over an hour, apparently. She isn't mad at Dora for what she did and Dora was so relieved by this she cried, both then and with me now. Watching her as she tells me all about the conversation with Esme, I can see this worry has been a physical burden on her, and the lightness of it having lifted from her shoulders is plain to see in her stature and face. It's terrific news, and obviously they are going to keep in touch.

'I shall look forward to hearing more on Saturday, then.'

'Oh yes. I will have more to tell you by then, I'm sure. I must get back as she said she would call again this week and I do not want to miss her.' As she makes her way back to her cottage, I'm not sure of the impact the counselling is having, but this one telephone call has put a bounce right back in her step. And distracted her enough she didn't even noticed I was off work.

I return to my spare room with a smile on my face as, brush in hand, I set about painting the woodwork.

I feel a considerable sense of accomplishment by the time I've finished. Delighted with my efforts and the difference they've made. There is the rest of the cottage to do, but that will have to wait.

Fiona calls at the end of the working day, and indeed working week, as the Easter weekend is upon us, to check in and see how I am. I mention some vague symptoms which show I am making progress. Everything is running smoothly, she reassures me, so I decide if I do get to return to Marchants, I shall maybe take more time off.

During the evening, I receive many thank you messages. Mr Marchant Senior was a kind man. He appreciated his staff, valued loyalty and wanted Marchant & Son to be a good place to work. He therefore went out of his way to treat his staff now and then. Naturally, I was the one to organise the treats, and they could be all manner of things. Trays of doughnuts or brownies delivered to the office and, of course, The Lodge. Sometimes we'd send treats to everyone's home: fruit baskets, gift cards, vouchers for the cinema, a turkey at Christmas, were some examples. For the last evening before this long weekend, I had arranged for beer, pizzas and Easter eggs to be delivered to all the employees. I hadn't exactly kept this a secret from Rex, I just hadn't told him, and as he paid scant attention to the accounts and had never questioned anything, to date I have got away with it. I suspect at some point he'll discover this expense and put a stop to it, which in my mind is short-sighted, as treats and events are great for staff morale.

Anyway, I receive many texts from appreciative staff, thanking me and hoping I am feeling better. It might be the company who pays for these treats, but all the staff know it is because of me that they get them.

I haul the furniture back into the spare room on Good Friday morning. I then spend the rest of the day attempting to clarify my thoughts. My physical endeavours this week have allowed me plenty of time to think. While my plans felt sketchy when I drove away from work on Monday, over the activity-filled days since, they have solidified and are coming together. Until now I haven't committed any of the detail to paper for fear once it's out of my head someone may discover it. Now I feel the need to write everything down, as having the details loose in my mind isn't giving me confidence I haven't missed something vital.

I therefore spend a couple of hours writing. What I've done. What I need to do. What I intend to achieve. Progress. Action. Outcome. I check and recheck my plans for areas of weakness. By the end of Friday evening, I am happy they are as solid as they are likely to get. I then go through my notes over and over, memorising every point. When I am confident I know exactly what I have to do, I burn the evidence in the kitchen sink.

Of course, for my plans to succeed, the order things unfold in is crucial. It is a situation like when you practise for one of those tough conversations you may have to have with someone. When you rehearse it, you imagine the person saying the right things in response to give you the outcome you want. The reality can be a far cry from what you planned.

Coffee and cake at Dora's is fun on Saturday morning because it is wonderful to see her so happy. Although I've been the one hoping to support her, it makes me laugh when I realise it's actually me who receives the respite I need from the stresses in my life at these get-togethers with Dora.

'Do you think you'll meet with Esme?'

'Oh, I hope so. I was going to offer to go up there, but before I could say anything, she mentioned coming here. I was thinking, as she is working, perhaps she could visit over one of those bank holiday weekends?'

'Good idea. There are a couple in May you could aim for, otherwise I think the next isn't until August. We have nowhere near as many here as we used to have when I lived in Spain.' I want to claw back the words the minute they leave my mouth.

She frowns. 'I never knew you lived in Spain.'

'No, well… I suppose we've never spoken about it, like much else,' and I raise my eyebrows at her, to which she can only manage a sheepish grin. 'It was years ago, anyway. My family moved out there when I was a child.'

'Are you fluent in Spanish, then?'

'I was. Not sure how I'd fare in a conversation now. There're not many opportunities to use it around here.'

She laughs and thankfully it is easy for me to switch the focus back onto Esme, her job as a primary school teacher, her wonderful Scottish accent, her husband who she clearly adores, the fact she has two children. Dora positively glows at being a grandmother.

I can barely get a word in edgeways from then on, and the good news is she is so consumed with Esme, she's forgotten about Spain, nor does it appear she's noticed I've been off all week so I have no awkward questions to answer there, either. The less lying I have to do, the better.

The other news from her is that as soon as her life has settled, she is going to apply to become a volunteer back at her primary school. Discovering that Esme is a teacher thrilled her, as they have something in common. So she wants to go and help in the classrooms, listening to children read or helping with craft activities. Wherever she's needed, she is happy to be. There is no mention of Amos at all, although I suppose that side of things is being dealt with in her counselling sessions. I imagine she won't want to taint her current happiness with thoughts of him.

On Sunday, Eddie calls me mid-morning to ask if I'm feeling better. When I say I am, he asks if it's convenient for him to bring the sleepers over. His truck pulls up outside a short while later.

'Happy Easter!' he says, as he hands me a large Easter egg.

'Oh! I wasn't expecting… I didn't get…'

'No worries,' he says. 'I suspected you are the sort of woman who would not have bought herself an egg. And everyone should enjoy some chocolate on Easter Sunday. I had mine for breakfast.'

'Breakfast?'

'Yup. Nothing like a whole egg to get you going on a Sunday morning. How are you doing? Better? You're looking great.' The high pitched sound of a motorbike as it travels through the village towards us distracts me from the compliment.

I've nearly forgotten I've been "ill". His call had reminded me earlier, so I swiftly respond with, 'Thank you. Yes, I'm better now. Raring to get back to work.' Then I turn in surprise as the motorbike appears and pulls into the kerb behind the truck.

Eddie raises his eyebrows, and gives me a smile, 'Sure you are. Now,' he turns towards the motorbike rider who dismounts with ease and removes his helmet revealing dark, shoulder-length hair and a youthful face, 'This is my nephew, Theo. He's come to lend us his muscles in getting this lot unloaded.' He gesticulates towards his truck, the back of which is filled with sleepers, a wheelbarrow strapped to the top.

'Thanks for your time, Theo. It's good to meet you.' I can see the family resemblance in his easy smile.

'No worries. Can't let the old man struggle on his own.' They both grin broadly and Eddie shakes his head at what is obviously an ongoing joke. I feel an unexpected pang for the lack of family in my life, then am shaken out of it by Eddie's next question.

'Do I take these through the passage to the side or round the back?' There is a gate at the end of the garden out into a lane, but it is narrow and parking can be an issue, so I rarely use it.

'The easiest route is through the passage. There's a pathway you can follow across the garden. I'll open the gate.' Minutes later, with the first sleeper balanced precariously on the barrow, they wheel it up and lay it against the wall.

'Would you like a coffee?' I ask as they walk back towards me.

'That would be grand. Milk and two sugars, please,' said Eddie.

'I'm fine, thanks,' says Theo, reaching to withdraw an energy drink from the side pocket of his trousers.

'You're not still drinking that rubbish, are you?' I hear Eddie say to him as they disappear down the passageway, but I'm unable to hear the response. I like their relationship and can feel the easy bond between them.

Once the coffee's made, I carry the mugs out into the garden. There is a pile of sleepers stacked already.

Eddie gratefully takes the mug from me. 'Thanks. Shall we have a quick measure up?' When I originally discussed the raised beds with him, I told him I wanted four. Now I'm concerned I've overestimated the size of the plot and they won't fit in around the existing fruit trees.

He takes out a tape measure and with Theo's help quickly puts my mind at rest. It's exciting now we're finally at the building point, and I can already imagine the beds full of fruit and vegetables over the coming months.

Once he's finished his coffee, Eddie and Theo get back to work. 'I'm going to the shop to get us some rolls for lunch,' I tell them as I carry the mugs inside.

'Will it be open on Easter Sunday?' says Eddie.

'I imagine so. Sharon's not one to miss an opportunity.'

'Don't get anything for me, thanks,' Theo says. 'I'll be off as soon as we're unloaded.'

It's a beautiful spring day. Blue sky, sunshine with the first heat of the year in it warm on my face, and the lightest of breezes. I try to enjoy the moment and push any dark imaginings of everything the next week could bring to the back of my mind. It isn't easy. The dark Rex-shaped cloud that hovers at the periphery of my mind threatens to take the edge off the joy of the day, but I keep beating it back while I can.

On the return journey I hear Theo's motorbike approach and wave as he passes. Once back home, I watch Eddie work as I put together a picnic lunch. Ham rolls with enough mustard to tickle the nose. Sausage rolls warm from the oven. Coleslaw, pickles and a salad. Toasted and buttered hot cross buns. I've bought some beer to offer to him.

I spread the feast on the garden table and call him over to join me. He's already made one bed and as he walks towards me I'm struck by how different he looks out of the scruffy work clothes I usually see him in. His blue checked shirt suits him and looks new, along with his jeans and boots.

'I haven't got far, I'm afraid.'

'Oh, you've done more than my George would have managed.' Eddie knows I was married so this mention won't come as a surprise.

'Not a handyman then?'

'Absolutely not. His talents lay elsewhere.' Eddie's eyebrows rise at my indiscretion.

'Intriguing. Are you still in contact?' This is awkward. If anyone ever finds out about George they assume we divorced and I correct that and say he died in an accident at work. However, there's something about Eddie, about our growing closeness that makes me want to tell him the truth, but I know it will only lead to questions I don't want to answer.

'Ah, no. He's, er, dead.' I clear my throat, the next truthful words poised, ready to spill out, but concern over what he'll think of me and my past stops them. The story I've given before has always been the easiest explanation. And it remains so. Even at this his face freezes.

'Shit. I'm sorry.'

'Don't be. You weren't to know and it was a long, long time ago.'

'Do you mind me asking what happened?'

'Of course not. It was an accident at work. A wrong place, wrong time kind of thing.' It's not a complete lie. I look away, brush a fly from my arm. 'It was devastating.'

'I'm sorry, I shouldn't have asked.' I know he has no idea what to say next so I help out.

'Of course you should have done. It was a long time ago and I've moved on. On which note,' and I indicate towards the picnic, 'I have beer? Or something soft?'

He smiles, probably with relief the subject's changed. 'I've had enough beer recently, thanks to you. I'm driving too so I'll have a soft drink if that's all right? It was an excellent pizza, too.'

'Glad you enjoyed it. It was a new supplier, so it's good to have the feedback. I'll get you a ginger beer instead.' I pop back inside to retrieve one from the fridge.

'What flavour did you have?' he asks when I return.

'Of what?'

'Pizza. Mine was a meat feast.' He notices my smile. 'But of course you already knew that.'

'I did.' I help myself to some salad and take a roll.

'So, what flavour did you have? I think you could be a ham and pineapple girl.'

'And what are your feelings towards pineapple on a pizza?'

'I'm ambivalent on the subject.'

'Good to hear, I'm all for an open mind, but I didn't have a pizza, or the beer, come to that.'

'Why not?' The crinkles at the corners of his eyes deepen.

'I guess I'm better at organising this stuff for other people and forget to include myself. Plus, when Rex finds out I do this, his anger will be ten times worse if he thinks I've taken advantage of it too.'

'How do you put up with him?'

'I've been wondering that myself.' I take a sip of ginger beer. 'Let's not talk about him today, though. It's too nice a day. Seen any decent series lately?' A long time ago Eddie and I discovered a shared interest in a good drama series. Crime, true or otherwise, police procedurals, psychological thrillers. Often the darker the better. We love them all and frequently recommend a recently discovered series to each other.

We spend a few minutes discussing the latest police procedural we'd both seen involving trafficking and domestic abuse survivors. It had been a harrowing if learning experience.

Eddie finishes his hot cross bun and downs the rest of his drink. 'Right, I must get back to work. I've only got today as the weather's going to break tomorrow. By the way, have you organised the topsoil yet?' I slap my hand to my forehead.

'No, I haven't.' Yet again, I feel a fool to be so disorganised with this project. Eddie is the driving force behind it and this is one more thing which has slipped my mind. What I am going to grow my vegetables in is anyone's guess, and I can only put my lapses in organisation down to all I've had on my mind recently. Or perhaps Rex has been right all along, and I am useless.

'Not to worry. I've got a friend who can supply a load.'

'Oh great. Which reminds me. What do I owe you?'

'You can have the sleepers at cost, same for the topsoil.' He withdraws a docket from his pocket and passes it over to me. 'I'll get you one for the soil.'

'Thanks, but what about for your time?'

'You're a friend. It comes free.'

'I can't let you do that.' He studies me for a moment.

'Okay, buy me a drink sometime.'

I nod, then busy myself gathering what remains of the picnic together, before adding, 'All right.' I try not to think on this too deeply and keep my thoughts strictly to this being a friend doing a friend a favour. But I can't deny that I feel ever so slightly giddy at the thought.

And I've moved on. That's what I said to Eddie earlier. It just came out and is the first time I've said it, or thought it. I consider the words for a while and wonder at the truth in them. Then find myself smiling.

Eddie was right. The rain rolls in during the early hours of the Bank Holiday Monday and I am glad to be inside. While thunderous clouds lie heavy over the land and rain falls in torrents, I try to burn off the nervous energy which builds throughout my body by cleaning my cottage ferociously throughout the day. By the evening, it's spotless, and I'm shattered. But it's no guarantee of a good night's sleep. I know my anxieties about facing the office, Rex, and the fallout of my actions will gather in looming, monstrous shadows, to darken the corners of my mind during the still, small hours of the night and chase away all chances of sleep.

12: My Trail of Breadcrumbs…

Despite being the one who set this ball in motion and also the one supposedly in control of said ball, I feel filled with trepidation as I drive to work. I know I could potentially be walking into a trap. During my time off, a thousand different scenarios have sprung to mind and in every one, Rex has discovered what I've done. Even now, I imagine him lying in wait, poised like a spider in a web. His car isn't in the car park, which means nothing. If he is planning on surprising me, he could have hidden it somewhere. Or got a lift. As I park, I consider what course I might have taken had my passport been valid, as hopping on a plane right now is most appealing.

While anxious about approaching the office building now, when I thought rationally over the last week, I was confident I hadn't been discovered and Rex wouldn't be at the office when I got there. He is late every day anyway, and as he is returning from holiday, and it is the first day back after a bank holiday, the best we can expect, based on his previous performance is that he puts in an appearance before the end of the day. Sometimes, he's not even bothered doing that.

All this means is that, if he is already here, it spells trouble.

Fiona has followed me into the car park and, thinking about there being safety in numbers, I wait for her to get out of her car and we walk towards the building together. A shower is petering out. Light drops sparkle like falling gems as the sun creeps from behind a purple grey cloud and a rainbow arches its way over the Marchant & Son building.

'Are you feeling better?'

'Much, thank you. Did you enjoy the long weekend?'

'Yes, it was wonderful. I hope yours wasn't spoiled by being ill. Are you looking forward to being back at work?' She laughs as I grimace. 'It never helps to have to catch up on everything when you get back to your desk, does it? It's the same when you take holidays. Makes you wonder if it's worth it. I hope I haven't left it in a mess.'

'I'm sure you won't have done. I've already dealt with some of the emails that came in. All those I could easily delete, anyway. You're never away from your desk nowadays, are you?'

'Unless you're Rex. He seems to manage it.'

'True. Maybe we should all be more Rex.' She laughs again.

'Don't even joke about it. Can you imagine!'

As we open the office, gathering the post and switching on lights, I cautiously scan the room as we discuss anything we need to progress this week. I take the bull by the horns and have a quick check in Rex's office, feeling a tremendous sense of relief once I can confirm he isn't lying in wait. Eventually, I get to my office and turn on my computer. As I take off my coat, I glance at the assorted piles on my desk and say, 'I'll reconnect the bank accounts to the system first so you can get caught up with the reconciliations.'

'Righto, I'll start with that.'

While I log in to the accounts system and re-authorise the bank accounts, the other staff arrive. Everyone checks in to ask how I'm feeling and it's great to hear the office alive with news of how everyone has spent the weekend. It's so different from the near silence we work in when Rex is here.

I sort out the post and take Rex's through to his office to place with all the rest. The pile isn't daunting. So many companies have gone paperless nowadays. I quickly flick through the envelopes to check there is nothing to alarm me and am pleased when I see only what I am expecting to see.

As I get back to my desk, Trish has kindly brought me a coffee, which is appreciated, and soon we are all busy with our various tasks.

From where I sit at my desk, I can't help but glance over at Fiona and can see her frowning at her screen. My heart beats faster as I wait for the next part of my plan to fall into place.

Not ten minutes later, she appears at my door. Keeping her voice low, she says, 'I think we've got a problem.' She clutches a printout of the bank transactions in her hand.

'What's the matter?'

'There's a large sum of money gone out of the account that I can't reconcile with any invoice paid.'

'Show me.' I hold my hand out for the paperwork. Fiona comes round to my side of the desk and points out five withdrawals, each for fifty thousand pounds. There is no name on the payment detail, only numbers.

I sit back in my chair and pretend to think as she takes the seat opposite. The colour has drained from her face, unsurprisingly. I try to appear similarly stressed. We've never had such a situation before.

I pull my keyboard towards me and log in to the bank. I print off the latest statement showing the payments in question. There is no more information on it than there was on Fiona's list of transactions from the software.

'Right. Let's think this through. Rex and I are the only ones with online access, and I know it wasn't me who moved the money.'

'But Rex was only here the day the first payment went out and he rarely gets involved in paying anything.' I rock my head back and forth.

'I know. But he has the ability to make payments, and he could have scheduled the other payments. Or, logged in from elsewhere.'

'Of course. But why would he take the money?'

'Why, indeed? Of course, it could be an outside party. Someone who's got into the account. That's my main concern.'

'Do we call the bank or the police?'

'Both, I think. We need to alert the bank there may have been some fraudulent activity on the account and try to find out more about the transactions and where the money went. And we need the police to be aware of the potential fraud as quickly as possible.'

'Should we wait until Rex gets into the office? He might know what it's about?'

'He might, but if he does, surely he would have already given us details of what those payments were for?' Fiona shrugs, knowing as I do what he's like with paperwork. 'The other thing is, we don't exactly know when he's going to be in. If there is a problem, and the money has been stolen, he wouldn't thank us for wasting time before reporting it.' I pause for a moment to take a breath. Then let it out to calm myself before I continue. 'I'll tell you what we'll do. I'll call Rex first to let him know what's going on, then I'll call the police. That gives him a chance to tell me if it is anything to do with him.

'Sorry to do this to you, but could you call the bank and query the transactions with them, please? You have the right security in place to do that.' Fiona nods but doesn't take back the list of transactions I hold out to her.

'I've got a copy of it so you can keep that one.'

'Thanks, and, Fiona, I think you'd better make your call from Rex's office. Let's keep this between us for now.'

'Will do.' She returns to her desk for the information she needs to make the call to the bank, and I push my office door to and call Rex on my mobile. As expected, it goes to voicemail. He never answers calls from me.

'Hello, Rex. I'm not sure when you're going to be coming into the office, but we have a problem here I need to alert you to. Someone has withdrawn a sizeable sum of money from the account. Two hundred and fifty thousand pounds. I'm assuming it's nothing to do with you or you'd have let me know as per company policy. Therefore, Fiona is calling the bank now and I'm about to call the police. Anyway, please call as soon as you can and we hope to see you in the office soon.'

Fiona has gone into Rex's office by the time I find the number for the police. It isn't an emergency, so 999 is out of the question and I'm not sure which number to call instead, so start with the main county force number.

'Hello, this is Alice Fraser. I work for Marchant & Son in Buntingley. I need to report something. Are you a police officer?'

'No, I'm a civilian police staff member. Can I ask the nature of the allegation please?'

'Of course, yes. It's regarding some money that's gone missing from our bank account.'

'Let me take some details. Confirm your name, please?' We then go through the laborious process of asking and answering a series of questions. Eventually, we get to the point of the call.

'You say money has gone missing from a business bank account? How much?'

'Two hundred and fifty thousand pounds.'

'Have you called the bank?'

'My colleague is doing so now and is on hold. We didn't want to wait around for their response before calling you.'

'Do you know who might be responsible for the crime?'

'Possibly. If it's not an outsider who's got into the account, it's probably Rex Marchant, my boss.'

There follows a further series of questions necessary to produce an incident log, I am told. While I am certain all the questions are important, they fill me with impatience. Why, I'm not sure, as it is hardly a situation in which the police racing here with their sirens blaring will gain anything.

'Can you tell me what the process is from here, please?'

'Yes, this incident log will go to a supervisor within the police control room and they'll make a decision on police deployment. You'll probably receive a call-back with a scheduled appointment time.'

'Okay, and will that be today?'

'Possibly. It will depend on workload.'

Once assured someone will call back and the police will attend the offices at some point, I go to check on Fiona. She is waiting in a queue to get to speak to someone at the bank. I tell her I've left a message on Rex's voicemail and update her on the situation with the police, then say I'll go and answer some emails until I hear anything further from them. I return to my office and try to settle to some work, but find it difficult to concentrate.

I attempt to put any imminent arrival of the police out of my mind, assuming it might be similar to the recent situation with the break-in when they arrived days later. To my surprise, I receive a call back within an hour, and am relieved when the scheduled appointment is for that afternoon.

The call ends, and I check on those working at their desks. I am going to have to say something to them or they're going to be in for a big surprise when the police arrive.

I leave my office and go towards the reception area. On the way, I tell each member of staff I need to have a few minutes of their time. Although it doesn't happen often, we hold any meetings in Rex's office, but as it's currently occupied by Fiona, this will have to do as I only need to say a few words. We are soon all gathered near Trish's desk.

'Fiona isn't here,' says Phil. 'I'm not sure where she's gone.'

'No, she's on the phone in Rex's office. But she's aware of what I'm about to say. This will only take a moment.' I take a deep breath and let it out. 'This is difficult to tell you, but we have a situation with some bank payment transactions we can't account for and I've called the police. Fiona is currently on the phone with our bank.' I look round at the anxious faces, but I'm not sure how to alleviate their worry. 'Hopefully there will be a quick resolution to the situation, but I wanted you to be aware because the police have scheduled an appointment with me at two o'clock this afternoon. Obviously, when they get here, we will give them whatever information they need. Okay?' There are nods all round. 'Does anyone have questions?'

'Does Rex know what's happened?' asks Phil.

'I've tried to ring him and had to leave a message so hopefully he'll listen to it soon and will come in. Maybe he'll make it in time for the meeting with the police, we shall see.'

'Will the police want to talk to any of us?' Trish asks.

I shrug. 'I don't know police procedure, so I'm not sure. Probably, but I think we'll have to wait for them.' I check with those around me expectantly, but there don't appear to be any further questions. 'Okay, everyone, back to work and try not to worry. I know this has come as a surprise, and my door is open if you need to talk.'

As they return to their desks, I turn to Trish. 'Are you okay?'

'Yes. I'll make sure I'm here when the police arrive.' She is pallid, her eyes wide.

'Don't worry, Trish. Because, unless you're the one who's got into our bank account, they're not coming for you.' She forces a smile in response to mine. I know she's a worrier, and my feeble attempt to lighten the mood is little help.

Fiona is still on hold and I can feel her frustration. She's never known anything different, but I fondly remember the days when the company had an allocated bank manager who we could call direct with any problem and who made you feel like a valued customer rather than an inconvenience, as it is nowadays. I tell her about the scheduled appointment and that I've informed and prepared the rest of the staff.

There has been no response from Rex to my message.

I return to my office and start on my emails. There are a lot, given I have all Rex's, too. I had checked there was nothing urgent among them while I was off, but keen to maintain the illusion I was too ill to come into work, I left all I could. Consequently, I now have many I can simply delete or reply to quickly and I swiftly whittle my inbox down to those needing a more considered response. There are a couple among Rex's emails I definitely need to bring to the attention of the police, too.

I ponder the contents of those emails for a while, impatient for the police to arrive as I want to get things moving, but watching the hands of a clock never encourages them to move faster.

Unsettled and finding it difficult to concentrate on work, I think back to when Fiona had come round to the cottage and warned me about the possibility of Rex bugging the office. I tend to agree with Phil and Fiona's views that he is somehow monitoring the computers. That thought was enforced when the email I hadn't copied him into appeared in my inbox once he'd left for his holiday. But I remember now she'd also suggested cameras might be installed and watching everything we did. I hadn't got around to considering this further because of Rex's unexpected departure and my "illness" but no sooner has it come back into my mind, than I become uneasy, convinced someone's eyes are on my every move.

What if Rex can see what I'm doing now? What if he's seen what I've discovered in his emails today? I don't know how to go about checking for trackers on my computer so I can do nothing to protect myself there, but I make a mental note to speak to Phil, away from the office, as soon as I can. There must be a way to get the computers checked.

Since discussing the possibility of there being bugs listening to us, Fiona and I have been careful not to say anything we shouldn't, but what about other surveillance equipment? What about cameras? Could they have been installed? I doubt Rex could have done it himself. He's never shown himself to be interested in tech, but it wouldn't have stopped him from arranging for someone else to do it. I take a casual look around without knowing what I'm checking for. With two of my office walls being glass, there is plenty of wall space where I'm sure it would be impossible to hide a camera.

Unable to settle to anything that requires concentration, I pick up a pile of filing which has built in my absence, and approach the shelves behind me. I haven't been able to do my usual check through the files so I do that now and, as I find the relevant file for each piece of paper, I take it off the shelf to insert the paperwork. As I do so I check each section of shelving for anything out of place. I find nothing. Deflated, I sit back in my chair and stare at the screen. If Rex is keeping an eye on us, I should at least appear to be working, so I get back to clearing out my inbox.

He's often called me a neat freak, as if it is a bad thing, because of the state of my office. It was more relaxed in his father's day, but back then I wasn't called upon to prove myself as I have to these days with his mother's spot checks. Now the files on my shelves are colour coordinated according to project and neatly labelled. They are all the same size and sit lined up like soldiers on parade. I've often considered the fact I could have some sort of obsessive thing going on because of how tidy everything has to be, and the systematic checking I do through the files each day, but I'm reassured as I'm not that way at home. While doing the filing though, I accidentally shifted the air freshener on the end of one of my shelves and it is now out of line. It irritates me I can see it from the corner of my eye as I delete a few more emails. I pause. It then takes everything I have to keep my gaze on the screen as the conversation I had with our cleaner Maureen a week ago floods back into my memory.

I know I was distracted at the time but I should have treated her words more seriously, considered the threat and removed the air fresheners immediately. I could kick myself that I didn't.

An image springs to mind of Abigail tweaking the position of the air freshener when she was last in. Is she in on it? Did she specifically move it to get a particular view? I look at where it sits on the shelf now and it points directly towards me sitting at my desk. I am both made to feel uncomfortable that it's trained on me, and relieved that it doesn't see where I go once I leave my office. That it won't have seen me enter Rex's that day.

Fiona exits from his now, and my thoughts evaporate once more. I notice several other members of staff also staring in her direction, the questions building in their minds.

She comes straight into my office, her face with no more colour to it than earlier. I point to a seat but say nothing as I reach under my desk to retrieve my waste bin. Her eyes widen as I stand, grab the air freshener, and drop it into the bin. I wink and tell her to stay put before I walk a quick circuit of the entire floor, collecting each of the air fresheners and adding them to the contents of my bin. There are six in total. Interestingly, there isn't one in Rex's office. Aware there are many eyes on me as I add each one to my bin, I end my route in the staff lounge where I find the final air freshener. I stand for a moment, not sure what to do with them. I don't want to leave them in the lounge. For all I know they might be recording sound as well as images, so will continue to spy, assuming they are the culprits, of course. I will investigate them further when I have the time to see if my suspicions are correct, but unable to take any chances, I want them out of the way. I briefly consider whether I'm being paranoid. Imagine if I'm completely wrong, and Rex had just done a positive thing for the office. No, I shake my head. I can't see it. If he had, why isn't there one in his office?

I walk back out of the lounge and towards the cleaner's cupboard. Opening the door, I see there is not a lot of room, but I reach past the floor cleaner and vacuum and plonk the bin right in the back corner. It's out of the way there and I take a folded tarpaulin off one of the shelves which line one wall and, with some difficulty, cover the bin with it. It will have to do until I have time to investigate the air fresheners more closely.

I return to Fiona, closing the door as I enter the office.

'You don't like the air fresheners?'

'I do. But I'm suspicious of them. I saw the cleaners one evening and thanked them for providing them and they said it was nothing to do with them. It was apparently Rex's doing.' Her eyes widen.

'Wow. And you think?' I nod.

'Yes, following on from what you said… actually, perhaps I'd better leave it there. In case the air fresheners turn out to be innocent.' Our conversation is in danger of verging on territory we don't want Rex to hear, so we revert to being careful about everything we say. I place my forearms on the desk and grasp my hands together, fingers threaded. 'So, how did you get on?'

'It's not great news, I'm afraid. The bank checked the information on the transactions at their end, but couldn't give me any further information on where the money went. They have logged our report of the missing funds and are currently treating it as a fraud. It will take further investigation, apparently.'

'Damn. How frustrating.'

'They said the police are the ones who can find out the information we want.'

'Okay, that's good.' I lower my voice. 'I'm intrigued why he's taken it, though?'

'Who?'

I mouth the word, 'Rex.'

'Oh, so you think…? I was going more with the idea of it being online criminals.'

'That may be the case, but then it occurred to me. If it was an outsider, why would they have stopped at two hundred and fifty thousand?' I shake my head. 'Surely they would have carried on and taken everything they could.'

'Good point.'

'The more I've thought about it, the more I'm certain.'

Fiona's voice is barely above a whisper. 'But if it was him, then surely there's less of an issue? It's his company, so presumably he can do what he wants with the money.'

'Not really. You can't just take whatever you want out of a limited company. Most of it was a deposit on the Scampton account, anyway. He must have seen it come in and taken each payment as it landed in the account. Plus, an additional fifty K besides. He can't play fast and loose with company money like that. How do we replace it?' While I keep my voice low, my frustration is obvious for Fiona to see.

'What about the police, though? If you think it's him should we cancel them coming as the money hasn't technically been stolen?'

'Hasn't it?' I make eye contact. 'There's more to this than we first realised.' I glance at the emails which had disturbed me earlier. Both are for flight bookings. I am about to point out the detail to Fiona when we become aware of the main office door opening as two uniformed officers enter. They speak to Trish, and she peers over in my direction. I raise my hand in acknowledgement. 'Let's see what the police make of this,' I say over my shoulder to Fiona as I make a move towards the door.

Police Constable Harris and Police Constable Dent introduce themselves and show me their warrant cards as I approach. 'I'm Alice Fraser. Mr Marchant's personal assistant.' It is the best description I can ever manage to describe my role. 'Shall we talk in my office?'

Every employee tracks our progress through the open-plan area. As we pass Fiona's desk, which she has returned to, I ask her to come in too, as I want her to be up to speed on the investigation. Once we are all seated and the door is closed, I introduce Fiona as my assistant and ask if anyone wants tea or coffee. Fiona then pops out to ask Trish to make coffees all round before returning.

'There's still a Mr Marchant here, then?' says PC Harris.

'Rex Marchant. Yes. But he's not here at the moment.'

PC Dent tilts her head and looks at her notebook. 'The information I have is that you believe two hundred and fifty thousand pounds has been taken out of your company bank account without authority. Is that right?'

'Yes, it is. But I think I know who's taken it.'

'We'll come on to that. Do you have proof of the withdrawals?' I pass her the bank statement with the payments clearly marked on it. As she studies the paper, I stare at the tight bun on the back of her head into which each hair is severely scraped, thinking the pressure on her scalp must be tremendous and painful.

'I know when I first called this morning, I said the money was missing from the account.'

'Are you about to tell me it isn't?'

'No, well, yes.' I can see Dent is struggling to remain patient. 'Fiona rang the bank at the same time as I called you. She had to hang on for ages to get through, but when she did, they couldn't give any further information about where it went. I was hoping you might have more success with finding out?'

'We can come to that later. You said you knew who had taken the money.'

'Oh, yes, I believe it was Rex, Mr Marchant. It's only he and me who have online access, and I know it wasn't me who made those withdrawals.'

'Someone else could have got into the account. Criminals, for example.'

'I suppose so. But how would they have known we had a fifty thousand daily withdrawal limit? And why would they have stopped at two hundred and fifty thousand?'

Dent inclines her head as if I've made a valid point. 'So, it appears Mr Marchant has allegedly withdrawn money from his own company bank account? Am I missing something?'

'It's not as simple as that. The money was essentially a client's deposit for their build and Rex shouldn't help himself to whatever he wants from the company account. But I need to show you something else.' I turn the screen on my desk round so both officers can see it.

Harris squints at the screen. 'What is it I'm looking at?'

'These two emails. Flight reminders.'

'I think you need to elaborate.' Trish pushes the door open to deliver the coffees, and I pause in my explanation until she leaves. It gives me a moment to take a breath and collect my thoughts. I'm anxious to get my point across clearly and without gabbling.

'Rex has been away for the last week. When he goes away, he diverts all his emails to my inbox. I was then off ill and only got back into the office today. I had taken no notice of the emails before because I assumed they were for a holiday, and I didn't open them until this morning.'

'And they're not for a holiday?'

'Not exactly, no.' I open each email so they can see the detail. 'This is a one-way flight from London to Istanbul. Then there's a second flight from Istanbul to Northern Cyprus.' There is a pause during which I'm not sure whether they are reaching the conclusion I want them to. I check my watch. 'The flight to Istanbul leaves in a couple of hours.'

Harris turns to his partner. 'What does Northern Cyprus mean to you, Dent?'

'No extradition treaty.'

'Exactly. Can you check it out?'

Dent takes a photo of the flight details with her phone. 'Is there somewhere private I can go?'

'Of course, Fiona, could you show PC Dent to Rex's office, please?' Moments later, Harris and I are alone in my office.

'When are you expecting Mr Marchant to be back in the office?'

'We don't know. He was due back from holiday yesterday, so he might be in later. Or he might not come in until tomorrow.'

'Not a hands-on sort of boss, then?' Fiona re-joins us.

'No, not exactly. I tried to call him earlier about the money but there was no answer and I left a message but he hasn't returned my call.' Harris lapses into silence. Is he connecting the dots or am I going to have to do it for him? Stolen money + missing boss + flights booked to a country with no extradition treaty = ? It's blindingly obvious to me. I glance at Fiona and am sure she has reached the same conclusion I have.

Rex's office door swings open and Dent is back with us before Harris has time to reply.

'I've made some calls. Rex Marchant has not checked in for the flight.'

'So that blows one theory then?' Harris had joined the dots, after all.

'Not quite. Because the flight to Istanbul was cancelled a short while ago. He'll have had to change his plans.'

Harris turns to me. 'Can you give me Mr Marchant's address please? And do you know where he's been on holiday for the last week?'

I am about to reel off his address, but something silences me. The something being Rex Marchant, who has just walked into reception.

He stares across at my office and we lock eyes through the glass. Seeing I have two officers with me and, given the message I'd left for him, he must know why. 'He's here. Rex has arrived.' I struggle to swallow as both officers stand and turn to look at him. I notice his hesitation before he walks towards us.

'Rex. Hello. Good holiday?' I say.

'Yes, thank you.' He avoids eye contact.

'Let me introduce you. This is PC Harris and PC Dent.'

He shakes hands with them. 'What's going on?' His question is to me as much as them.

'Didn't you get my message?' It would be like him to not have listened to it. But I can't believe he has walked in here with no idea what's happened.

'Yes.'

'But you didn't think to reply?'

'I was on my way here already, so there wasn't any need. Besides, I'm sure you have it all in hand.'

'There wasn't any need? Or perhaps it's becau—' Dent raises her hand, which is all it takes to interrupt what was about to be an accusation and the potential ruin of her approach.

'Let's take a minute, shall we?' Dent says, as Rex and I glare at each other. 'Mr Marchant, could you sit please as we have some questions which might help clear all this up?'

'Rather than questions, how about some answers? What's being done to find the missing money?' He looks from Fiona to me. 'What did the bank say? Heads will fucking roll if you've allowed my money to be stolen.' He thrusts his index finger in my direction, just so it is completely clear who he has in his sights.

'I don't think there's anything to be gained by throwing around accusations, Mr Marchant. Especially as we already have an idea who took the money.' There's a beat. A silence.

'Of course we do. It's her.' His sausage-like finger points in my direction again.

My intake of breath earns me a warning glare from Dent, and I hold back my response.

She then goes on to patiently reply, 'Ms Fraser has informed us it's only you and she who have online bank access. Is that correct?'

'Yes.'

'She also tells me she didn't take the money.'

'She's lying, because I didn't, so it could only have been her.'

Dent contemplates his reply briefly, then changes tack. 'Talk me through your movements today, Mr Marchant.' Rex's brow furrows.

'I got up, showered and came here.'

'Considering it's past lunchtime, it would indicate you didn't get up that early?'

'I was still in holiday mode.'

'Perhaps you were in fact planning on going somewhere else today, instead of into the office?'

'No…' The word is drawn out as though Rex is questioning where this is going.

'Not to the airport, perhaps?'

'No.' There's surprise in it this time.

Dent reaches over to turn my screen so it faces the other side of the desk. She asks me to open the emails containing the flight details. I do, and Rex's bafflement increases as he reads them. I know at some point Dent will stop this discussion and take Rex to the station for formal questioning. Therefore, I make the most of lapping up every delicious second of Rex's discomfort while I can. Harris had pulled his chair back to remove himself from the immediate discussion and remains quiet, watching.

Rex holds out his hand towards the screen, palm uppermost. 'I have no idea what this is about.'

'It appears you have booked yourself onto two flights. The one to Istanbul scheduled for today. The second one on to Northern Cyprus for tomorrow.'

'Why would I have done that? It makes no sense?'

'Do you understand the implication of this trip?'

'No.'

'Have you heard of extradition treaties?'

This time Rex nods. 'Yes.'

'What is an extradition treaty?'

'It's where two countries have an agreement where they can get another country to send back someone they suspect of being a criminal.'

'Exactly. And do you know what's special about Northern Cyprus?'

'No.' The short word is laden with the apprehension in Rex's voice. He's perched on the edge of his seat.

'There is no extradition treaty between the UK and Northern Cyprus.' I can almost hear Rex's mind whirling with confusion in the silence that follows. We all wait for his response.

'Right. And you think I took the money and was going to run away? To Northern Cyprus?' Dent merely tilts her head in acknowledgement. 'Look, I didn't book these flights and surely the fact I didn't go to the airport to get on the first one proves I knew nothing about them?'

'It proves nothing of the sort. No one could contact you. You didn't reply to an urgent message left for you by Ms Fraser. Not until the flight was cancelled did you show up here as if nothing had happened, claiming you're innocent.'

'Seriously? I am innocent. You think I'd go on the run for a measly quarter of a mill?'

Dent's eyebrows rise. 'In my experience, people have done far more for much less, Mr Marchant.' I can see the panic in Rex's eyes.

'Someone has done this. Someone has set me up,' he blurts, then turns his attention to me and rises from his seat. 'You. It was you, you vindictive bitch!'

'Steady,' Harris commands.

'I have done nothing but get on with running the company in your absence.' Keen to maintain a cool professional demeanour, I am determined not to rise to his anger or accusations.

'But you could have arranged all this. Made the bookings and done the transfers. All of it.' He faces Harris, but while he speaks to him, he points his finger directly at me. 'You need to investigate her.' Rex gulps and lowers himself back into his chair. He takes a deep breath to compose himself. Then places both hands, fingers splayed, on my desk, bows his head and takes a moment before he raises it again, staring Harris straight in the eye. 'Investigate her, please. She could have taken the money as easily as me. But I know I didn't do it.' He pleads with the fervour of a condemned man, while I say nothing in my defence, happy to let the evidence unfold and speak for itself.

13: The Unexpected Turn of Events

PC Harris nods at his partner and leaves the room before speaking into his radio. He is back moments later. 'I've called for back-up.'

Rex leaps to his feet and throws my office door open before storming to his own, pursued by both officers and me.

'Mr Marchant, you can't be in here,' says Dent.

'Why not, eh? It's my office. I have every right.'

'This is now a crime scene. I can't allow you to remain in here, sir. You might disturb or tamper with evidence crucial to the case.'

'You're on her side then, are you? You believe her lies?'

Harris raises his hands to defuse the situation. 'We're not on anyone's side. Ms Fraser's office is also a crime scene. We'll take your computers for analysis and hopefully they'll reveal the truth of what's happened. Is there somewhere else we can go for now?'

'Where's your warrant, eh? You'll be taking nothing without one of those.' He sounds pathetically entitled and isn't thinking rationally.

I can't help myself. 'If you're innocent, Rex, the computers will prove it. Why are you getting in the way of that?' He fixes me with a look of pure venom.

Harris says, 'We don't need a warrant in this instance. The necessary items will be taken under our search and seize power.'

'There's a lounge for the staff we could use,' I inform the officers.

'Show me.' I lead the way when Harris herds us out, while Dent stays behind to presumably guard the entrances to our offices. I check across the open-plan section at the rest of the staff, who are watching every move we make.

'Does anyone want a tea or coffee?' I ask as Rex, silent now, sinks into the corner of the sofa, a frown on his face. Harris declines my offer, not having drunk the one brought to my office earlier. Rex doesn't respond and as neither tea nor coffee is going to be strong enough for me right at this moment, I leave it too. 'What's going to happen now?' I ask. 'Will we be able to get back into our offices later?'

'Possibly.' Harris then turns to Rex. 'Mr Marchant, I am arresting you on suspicion of fraud. You do not have to say anything. But it may harm your defence if you do not mention when questioned something which you later rely on in court. Anything you do say may be given in evidence.'

Rex nods, his face ashen. After clearing his throat, he says, 'Should I call my solicitor?'

'If you think you need one. You will be advised on your rights at the station, but you can make your call now if you prefer.'

I assume he'll call his solicitor direct, but he doesn't. He calls his mother. Of course he does. She'll sort it all out for him, as always.

Harris is speaking again. 'Alice Fraser, I am arresting you on suspicion of fraud. You do not have to say anything. But it may harm your defence if you do not mention when questioned something which you later rely on in court. Anything you do say may be given in evidence.'

Not part of the plan.

I suppose I should have been prepared for this eventuality, but I'm not. Naively, I hadn't considered it as an outcome. My stomach lurches as my breaths become shallow and I collapse onto the nearest chair, my legs unable to hold me any longer.

This is it then. The unexpected turn of events. The outcome that doesn't care how much planning you've done, and the reality that can be a far cry from what you've prepared for.

I remain silent. I have no solicitor on speed dial, no mother I can call for help, so I decide to wait and see what I'm told at the station. PC Harris remains with us in the lounge, speaking occasionally into his radio, but I can't make out what he says above the roaring in my head. Half an hour passes before PC Dent comes in and says it's time to go. Harris takes out his handcuffs. Heat flushes my cheeks. The shame. I don't think I can bear it.

'They won't be necessary, surely?' I say, my voice quiet. Harris looks from me to Rex.

'Maybe not for you.' His voice fades as his eyes remain on my boss. Given the evidence he's seen so far I can see he has reason to be concerned Rex might attempt an escape, but with the effort it takes for him to get up from the sofa, he doesn't appear as though he'll be running anywhere, anytime soon.

'Oh, don't you worry. I'm going nowhere until you've sorted this mess out and locked that bitch up.'

We walk out of the lounge. Harris first, then Rex and I, and Dent, follow. I notice two new uniformed officers standing outside the doors to my office, and Rex's. My cheeks burn and I can't bear to make eye contact with anyone as we pass. But I sense their eyes on me, which only intensifies my humiliation.

We are driven in separate cars to the station and after processing I find myself in an interview room, alone. I suppose it's better than a cell, which is what I had been expecting. When offered, I decline the services of a duty solicitor, at least for now. I'll see how the interview goes as I was told I can ask for one at any time.

I've been incredibly stupid. With us being the only two with online access to the bank account, of course I should have anticipated my arrest and expected to be treated as a suspect and I can't believe I didn't give the possibility proper consideration. Now it has happened, it is fine. I keep telling myself that. It is part of the process. While waiting, I've calmed and know what I need to do.

I am curious about where Rex is in the building. Is he also in an interview room? Is he already being interviewed? I grow twitchy at not knowing what is going on with him and regret turning down the offer of a solicitor. I know Rex will have one. An expensive one. One that might get him preferential treatment? Would the police allow that?

I worry about all those left at work. About how they are getting on and what they are thinking. If they are even still there, of course. Would the police have sent everyone home while they did their, what did they call it? Search and seize? That was it. I don't know if they will close off the entire building. And if they do, for how long? How will we keep Marchant & Son going if we can't get into the offices? These thoughts, along with many others, chase around my brain as I wait. And wait.

While I contemplate how long I will be detained, the door opens and a man and woman, both dressed in plain clothes, enter. He introduces himself as Detective Sergeant Barker, the investigating officer appointed to this case, and his colleague as Detective Constable Wilson.

I have seen enough police dramas to know they will record the interview, the introductions and preliminaries familiar.

'While you remain under arrest, you are also the complainant, so we need an initial statement from you.'

The interview that follows is a straightforward retelling of the events which have occurred so far. DS Barker is a man with a sharp eye for detail, which I appreciate and give him everything I can. He's keen-eyed and eager, and I get the impression little gets past him. I leave emotion out of it and he doesn't ask about my relationship with Rex. Our case is going to be one of he said/she said and my chief concern is I'm not sure how seriously they will take the word of an employee against that of the boss. At some point, when they make further investigations, they are bound to expand that to disgruntled employee and it will only sway matters further in Rex's favour. Therefore, I now feel strongly I need to get out all the points I have to make now.

In my mind, the outcome will entirely hinge on any evidence discovered, and this will most likely come from the computers. The additional officers that were present as we walked out had clearly been there to preserve the crime scene, and I want to know what the process is from there. I can't remember any crime show I've seen being about financial crime. It simply isn't as interesting for the viewing public as the murders and catalogue of human misery generally served up. Harris had said they will take the computers for analysis. But as for anything else they might take? I don't know.

I'm not sure if I'm allowed to ask anything, but when I feel the interview is coming to an end, and with no solicitor to advise me differently, I do so anyway.

'Can you tell me what happens now? What investigations you'll be doing?'

'We'll carry out interviews with the other members of staff at the offices over the next day or so. Make contact with the bank. And we'll be ascertaining whether the computers can give us any initial findings.'

'Do I stay here while you do that?'

'No. We'll release you on bail.'

'What does that mean?'

DC Wilson clarifies, 'There will be conditions. You'll have to surrender your passport–'

'Mine's expired.' I'm pleased to get that in. To me, it strengthens my case. Makes it clear I am unable to run away.

'We have your home address, which we assume is where you'll be staying.' I nod. 'And you'll have to sign in at a police station a few days a week, but we'll advise you further when you're released.'

'Will you be releasing Rex too?'

'Probably.'

'Can I go back to the office?'

'Do you want to?' DS Barker frowns.

'Despite what Rex thinks, the business doesn't run itself. There are a lot of staff whose livelihoods rely on it.'

'Once we have finished gathering evidence, you can go back in.'

'Do you need any of the contact details we have for the bank? I can get those for you.'

'No need. I'm an accredited financial investigator. That gives me direct access to any financial institution.'

'Oh. I wish I had that kind of clout with the bank.' He smiles briefly at my pathetic joke before ending the interview.

A short while later, I walk out of the custody suite. It is a little after nine and dark. I fumble my phone out of my pocket to call a taxi, debating whether to go straight home or collect my car first, then remember I have the keys for neither. Both are in my handbag next to my desk, along with the set for the office. I'd been so upset when cautioned I didn't even think to bring it with me. Who will have locked up? Or are the police still stationed there? I stop, unsure what to do next, then relief floods through me as I see Eddie leaning against the bonnet of his truck, ending a call on his phone.

Without a word, he opens the passenger door and ushers me in.

'Thank you. How long have you been waiting?'

'A while.'

'I'm sorry to have put you out.'

'It's fine. I didn't want you to come out of there and not have someone waiting. Home?'

'Yes, please. My neighbour has an emergency set of keys.'

'Uh huh. How did it go?'

'I think it was all right. A Detective Sergeant Barker interviewed me and we went over what had happened. It was straightforward. I'm more worried about what Rex has been saying. He's determined to pin the blame on me.'

'The police will see through his lies. We've seen enough shows to know that,' he says, and grins over at me.

'That's true. But Rex will have his fancy solicitor by his side. Maybe I made a mistake by not asking for a duty solicitor.'

'If it's any consolation, I was in the car park for a while and didn't see Rex leave the building.'

'Oh. Interesting. I'd assumed his solicitor would have him back home and tucked up on the sofa by now.' Eddie chuckles. I gaze out of the side window as we enter Melton and murmur almost to myself, 'I wonder what he's telling them.'

We draw to a stop in front of my cottage and, somewhat surprisingly, behind my car.

'How did that get here?'

'You don't realise how many friends you have.'

The lights in my cottage are on, the curtains drawn, and I've never seen a more welcome sight. Fiona opens the front door. I could sob when I walk in to find Phil about to serve pasta into bowls as Fiona pours a bottle of red into glasses.

'Thank you.' Their kindness humbles me.

We pull my table out and sit round it. The kernel of the Marchant family.

'This is delicious, Phil. I think you're wasted as a project manager.'

'I'm an enthusiastic amateur, that's all. I find it relaxing.'

'And I get to enjoy the output.' Fiona grins as she gazes fondly at him. Nothing further needs to be said to explain their relationship.

I raise my glass and toast my friends before moving on.

'What's the situation at the office? Have they closed down the entire building?'

'No, it's all fine. They determined the two offices as the crime scene and isolated those. We could all carry on as normal,' Fiona rolls her eyes, 'although I'm not sure how much work got done from then on.' She glances at Phil, who shakes his head.

'It was difficult to do anything with so many distractions,' he adds. 'A while after you left, two detectives arrived.'

'Dent and Harris didn't come back then?' Fiona shakes her head.

'No, it was a Detective Sergeant Barker, and Detective Constable Wilson.' She checks her phone where she'd made a note of the names.

'They're the ones who interviewed me.'

'Okay, so they were at the office for a while. We could obviously only see what they were doing in your office, but they checked through the drawers and some files. Leafed through your diary. Then Phil thinks, well, you tell them.'

'Another team arrived,' he says.

'Scenes of Crime Officers?' Eddie asks.

'No, there was no forensic evidence gathering. I think these were specially trained officers from hi-tech crime. I did a bit of googling,' he adds by way of explanation. 'They dealt with seizing Rex's and your computers, but they also checked out the internet routers and all network devices plus the CCTV.'

'Are we without internet access then?' I ask, as it's a situation we'll have to rectify quickly.

'No. Eventually, they only took the two computers.'

'Anyway, once they were there and dealing with that, Barker and Wilson told us they'd be back in the morning to take statements from everyone. That must have been when they came back to interview you.' Fiona punctuates this by refilling glasses.

'And you were then allowed back into Rex's and my office?'

'Yes. Which is how I could retrieve your handbag,' she says, pointing to where she's left it on the side.

'Thank you for bringing my car home, and all this…' I indicate round the table. 'I was not expecting to come home to quite such a welcome.'

'We were happy to help,' says Phil.

I turn to Eddie. 'What does anyone know at The Lodge?'

'Not much. Although the rumour mill is in full swing.'

'Okay, so someone had better fill them in. I'll come in early tomorrow to speak to them. Try to slow down the gossip. Or Rex can do it if he prefers.' All laugh out loud at this suggestion.

'He may not even be out of police custody by then. They can keep you for twenty-four hours without charging you, you know,' Phil adds.

'Then I'll consider myself lucky to have got off so lightly,' I say, and drain my glass. Privately, I caution myself against getting cocky. This is only the first day of the police investigation. I'm already surprised by my arrest, who knows what may follow?

After the others leave, I lock and bolt the doors and windows. Then double-check them before I shower, keen to get the pervading scent of the custody suite off me and, exhausted, I fall into a restless night of broken sleep and vivid dreams which evaporate as I wake, startled by the first bird chirp of the new day.

I lie there for a while and consider my options. Given the choice, I don't want to go into the office now that I've slept, albeit fitfully, on all that has happened. My primary concern is bumping into Rex. I don't want to have to deal with the confrontation. But I'd stated last night I'd go in to talk to all those who work out of The Lodge, so have to stick to my word.

I rise and groan, wondering how all the onsite staff wake at this time every day.

I take a long route round to the office, stopping in at a twenty-four-hour supermarket to buy a substantial quantity of freshly baked sausage rolls and pastries. The smell which fills my car as I drive on is intoxicating, although my appetite evaporates on the approach to Marchant & Son.

There is no sign of Rex's car.

I walk round to The Lodge. Inquisitive faces from those getting out of work trucks turn in my direction, I smile and indicate we should all enter the building. Those who were out on site the previous day could hardly have missed the fact something was going on, as the car park had had several police vehicles in it, together with an officer on the main door managing all who entered, so I'd been told. Eddie said gossip is rife, so with eager faces all round as everyone crams into the largest room, it's only fair to put them in the picture. The murmur of voices rises as we wait for the stragglers, although those present fall upon the food I've brought with appreciation and as though they haven't eaten in weeks.

Eddie walks over to stand next to me. 'Did you get any sleep?'

I smile up at him. 'A bit. Not enough.' He inclines his head to those in the room.

'They're intrigued. Mostly by Rex's absence.'

'Surely they can't be surprised. He's never in the office on time, let alone early.'

'Ahh, but the office is a different world to out here. We don't know half of what goes on, or how he behaves.'

'Lucky you.'

He then lowers his voice to a near whisper. 'Just to warn you, some of the gossip has been extreme. If I believed half of it, I'd have been in touch to ask if you needed me to hide the body? I do have several excellent locations in mind.' My tension releases as my cheeks stretch in a smile, then I laugh briefly.

'Unnecessary right now. But good to know for the future.'

'You never know what sort of mess you're going to get yourself into, so the offer is always there.' I grin at him again, then face the room and call for quiet.

'I know there's been a lot of talk and some of you are aware of the police activity yesterday. This meeting is to bring you all up to speed and answer questions.' I look round the room before I continue. 'Early yesterday Fiona alerted me to the fact some money had gone missing from the company bank account. Obviously, we called in the police and contacted the bank. The subsequent activity in the office has been disruptive for all working in there and no doubt rumours have spread to the staff here. I'm sorry I couldn't speak to you all earlier, as it must have been a worrying time. But, let me reassure you the business of Marchant & Son will continue as usual.' There is a definite release of the tension in the room. I haven't had time to adequately plan what I'm going to say and am interrupted as I marshal my thoughts.

'How much did they take?'

'A quarter of a million.' There is an intake of breath, a low whistle.

'Was it scammers? Did someone click on one of those dodgy links?' Noise builds immediately as some begin arguing about how stupid you'd have to be to fall for one of those scams. I can see this could quickly descend into chaos if we go off track.

Then one of the younger roofers, Dean, calls out, 'Where's Rex? Why isn't he in front of us now?'

I raise my hand and call for quiet again. 'I can see I need to tell you more before you all start speculating and spiralling into a rabbit hole of conspiracy theories. At the moment, this is only what *appears* to have happened, as the police investigations are at an early stage. The money went out of our account with little information on where it had been transferred to. The police are contacting the bank about what's happened and tracking where it has gone.' You could have heard a pin drop in the room.

'Rex and I are the only ones with online access to the bank account. Both of us deny taking the money, so I guess it could be criminals or scammers. At the moment, I know nothing more about that. The police have taken away our computers, which they will examine to see if they reveal anything to show what's happened. Along with other investigations they'll be carrying out.'

'I heard you were arrested.' Dean again. I swallow.

'Yes, both Rex and I were arrested yesterday. I alerted the police to the issue, but as both of us have access to the bank account, of course, their actions were understandable.' I say this now as comfortably as if I'd been expecting it when in reality it had come at me like a lightning strike. 'They questioned me yesterday before bailing me.'

'Will Rex also be out on bail?'

'I assume so, but have no confirmation of that. I'm expecting him to make contact today.'

More information will come out in due course, so once I quieten them again, I tell them we'll update them when we can. In the meantime, I want us all to carry on with our work as usual.

The noise rises again and Eddie walks out with me.

'Are you okay?' he asks.

'Yes,' I say, as brightly as I can. 'Although I could have done without all this.'

'I can imagine. Can I do anything to help today?'

'Could you keep an eye on things here and let me know if any issues arise among the guys that we need to deal with? Questions they might have, that sort of thing?'

'Of course.' He's carried on walking with me right round to the main door of the office. I reach into my bag for the keys. 'I'll stay here with you until some others arrive.' His manner is nonchalant, but appreciated. The major fear I am bound to have to face today is meeting Rex. Doing so alone is unthinkable.

I switch on the lights and look across to my office, my desk strangely empty.

We walk over and stand in the doorway, and while I know Eddie will obviously notice what is missing, I can see beyond to the fact the entire room appears in disarray, as though every drawer, every file has been rummaged through. The feeling, this intrusion into my personal space, produces in me must be similar to, although a pale comparison with, what people experience when returning to their burgled home. It's ironic it has been the police who have left me feeling so edgy and uncomfortable, and I know I am going to have to put everything straight before I'll feel settled in here again.

Barker questioned me at length about the processes in the office and company policy. He'd wanted to know how everything worked. Who was responsible for what? Who had keys to the building? Which areas the CCTV covered? Who had what level of authority for bank access and online payments? He'd asked how we logged in to the computer system and the bank? Where we kept that sensitive information and who had access to it? Fortunately, because I am particularly tight on that type of security, he appeared satisfied with what I told him. All the time we were talking, I could see his mind ticking over as he tried to fit all the pieces together. I am confident everything I said will agree with my records kept here. My only hope now is that the investigations carried out on the computers will tally with what I told him, too. I'm not sure I'll be able to breathe deeply again until I know they do.

The reception door opens behind us and we turn to see Fiona and Phil. Trish follows soon after.

'I think my work here is done and I can leave you in safe hands,' Eddie says, smiling before he walks away. He greets the others cheerfully as he leaves, and weirdly, considering I am no longer alone, I experience the strangest pang of loss the minute he steps out of the door.

'We came in early to prepare for the police arriving,' Fiona says as she reaches me, dumping her bag and coat on her desk. 'Any news on Rex?'

'Not a word. I'll ask the police for an update when they get here.' I'm keen to make a start on sorting out my files, but want to make sure everything is in place for them first. 'Shall we go and check out Rex's office? They can take statements with complete privacy in there.' Even though I know he isn't in there,

I don't want to enter alone and, ridiculously, I find myself opening the door tentatively in case he is about to spring out and surprise me.

While Fiona sets out the desk area, I check the kitchenette has everything that will be needed, restocking where necessary. I prepare the coffee machine, fill the kettle and set out plenty of cups and saucers together with biscuits.

DS Barker and DC Wilson arrive shortly after nine. I meet them in reception.

'Ms Fraser. You couldn't keep away then.'

'No. I wanted to make sure everything was ready for you. We've put you in Rex's office. I hope that's all right?' I say this over my shoulder as I'm already leading the way. 'We've arranged refreshments for you, but let me know if there's something missing, or if you'd prefer for one of us to deliver drinks to you. That'll be no problem. I'm not sure how you normally work.' I am disturbingly nervous and know I'm talking too fast, but cannot stop.

Barker brings up his hand as though to interrupt my flow. 'This is great. We rarely get treated so hospitably.'

'Oh, good.'

Fiona walks in and hands a clipboard to DC Wilson.

'There's the list of employees you wanted. The first page lists all those who work in here, the back lists those out at The Lodge.'

'Super, thank you.' Feeling superfluous, I mutter I'll go and get on, then hear Fiona ask if they want her to send people through. The door swings closed behind me before the answer comes, but I'm happy in the knowledge it's unlikely I'm going to have to have another session with them today.

14: A Warring Couple

Fiona had walked in as I was about to ask about Rex, which distracted me from doing so, but as the two officers running the investigation are here, I can only assume they've questioned Rex and released him. I don't think the police would have had enough to detain him overnight, anyway. This realisation concerns me and is behind the flutter of nerves in my stomach because I don't know where or when he'll pop up next.

Despite recent evidence to the contrary, I do not like confrontation and I know I'm probably going to have to face it today. I'm also uneasy about how the police presence over the next few days will go. Whereas I had simply shared the facts while being interviewed, I know Rex will have consistently accused me during questioning and told them all about our difficult relationship. Has he done enough for the police focus to swing further in my direction? If so, what might their next action be?

Before going back to my office, I go to check on Trish, who is behind the reception desk.

'How are you?' she asks.

'Fine, thank you. And you?' She might have replied she is all right, but her pale, solemn face and the shadows beneath her eyes tell me different. Having witnessed what occurred yesterday, she is no doubt concerned about what today will bring. She grimaces, then says, 'I'm a bit nervous about giving a statement.'

'Oh, don't be,' I reassure her in as easy breezy a fashion as I can manage. 'The officers are fine, so answer any questions they have and I'm sure you'll be out of there in a jiffy.'

Her expression relaxes marginally as she says, 'I hope so.' She then has to answer the phone, so I return to my office.

It isn't Trish I'm worried about. Or Fiona. Although she knows most about what has gone on. It's Phil, and by default, Eddie.

Phil is the only one who I asked to do something to enable me to do what I needed to. What if, when questioned, he reveals the fact I'd suggested he get Rex out to The Lodge to meet with Eddie over plans that didn't need discussing? It may be enough to distract the police from looking in the direction I want them to.

I can't bring myself to ask him not to mention it. Or to lie. The same goes for Eddie.

As I realign my files then rearrange the contents of the drawers in my desk, I dwell on this, but as I've resigned myself to doing nothing about it I try to dispel it as a worry which will simply have to play out.

Once I've finished straightening my office, I'm more at ease and check through my diary for what I need to get done. I still keep a wire-bound, and according to Rex "old-fashioned", paper diary which lies flat on my desk, and I'm thankful I do as it has all my reminders in it. I run my finger down the list of tasks but as when there is a power cut and everything you think of in order to pass the time – have a cup of tea, watch a film – involves using electricity, I find each item in the diary requires some element of me needing to use the computer. We have all our files backed up online, and I consider whether Rex and I should buy a couple of computers to see us through until we get our own back, but it feels excessive for what could turn out to be a short-term need.

It then dawns on me I could have brought my laptop in from home and used it for this interim period. I don't know why I didn't consider this option earlier. My only excuse being, with everything going on, I'm hardly thinking straight. But it is a solution, and I'm sure Phil can help me get everything on it that I need. For today, though, I continue to deal with emails on my phone, squinting at the screen as I do so.

Fiona has gone in first to be interviewed and hers is the longest of the day, although I try not to clock-watch. Trish's is shorter. Phil's is the most agonising for me to be patient through. Once he comes out, I half expect Barker to call me to in answer more questions but to my relief he doesn't. Although that may not mean anything. Wilson keeps coming out and calling in each member of staff while I busy myself.

I'd asked Trish to arrange for a local bakery to deliver a selection of cakes here and to each of our building sites mid-morning, and when they arrive, I go round to make everyone a tea or coffee as they are being more productive than I can be right now. Between interviews, I take a couple in for Barker and Wilson and manage not to ask how it is all going. Even though I am desperate to know what people are saying.

For the first time I can sympathise with Rex's, still to be proven, need to spy on us. It is frustrating not to be on top of everything happening in the company. But there is a world of difference between wanting to do something and actioning that desire.

Barker and Wilson walk out of Rex's office mid-afternoon.

'Have you finished?' I say, when Barker appears in my doorway.

'For now. We'll come back if we need to speak to anyone else.' They haven't interviewed anyone from The Lodge, I note. 'Thank you for being so cooperative and for all the hospitality. We appreciated it.'

'You're welcome,' I say, and stand to show them out.

Rex arrives within ten minutes of them leaving, which immediately tells me they'd called him. Another thing to make me uneasy. While my mind jumps to the conclusion, it is an overly friendly call for them to make. When I'm thinking more rationally, it makes sense they would have arranged with him to use his office for the interviews, rather than drag everyone down to the police station. It is therefore also perfectly reasonable they would call him once they had finished for the day. I need to keep my paranoia in check.

His mother is with him; I understand his need for moral support, and neither speaks one word to anyone as they walk through the open-plan section. I don't even glance in their direction as they pass because I've decided not to engage unless either makes the first move.

Which he does.

Unable to restrain himself, no sooner has he entered his office than he exits it again at speed, swinging through my door. He towers over my desk, then plants both hands on it and leans towards me. His face is flushed, a vein raised on his temple.

'How dare you steal from me!'

'I haven't—'

'Don't lie. I've been humiliated and questioned because of you.' I stand, wipe away the drop of his saliva that landed on my cheek, and lean towards him.

'So have I, because of you.' This time it's me pointing the finger.

Abigail is at his side, pulling at his arm. 'You were told not to speak to her, Rex. Come away.' She stares at me, her lip curled in a snarl. 'She's not worth it.'

He throws up his arms. 'I can't just do nothing but wait for the police to do something!'

'You can and you will.' Abigail's tone brooks no opposition.

She turns to me. 'You will get what's coming to you.' With that she pushes Rex firmly towards the door.

I'm left as though frozen in place. I sit, shaken, and clasp my hands together to still the tremor.

Our relationship appears to have descended to that of warring couples who separate but for financial reasons have to remain in the same house. It is going to be a deeply unpleasant time ahead.

Fiona rushes over, 'Are you okay?' I can only nod as I struggle to swallow. 'That was brutal.' She stares at his office door. 'Makes you wonder what he's capable of.'

'I know,' I murmur. I am afraid of him, although I can't voice as much. His anger is growing as the pressure mounts and I'm not sure how much more he can take before he spirals out of control.

Fiona sits with me for a few minutes. Makes us both a cup of tea, in true British style, as I plaster on a stiff upper lip and pretend all is well.

What Rex and Abigail are doing in his office, other than reclaiming it, I don't know. But whatever it is, it doesn't take long as, on the stroke of five when everyone else is only thinking about closing down for the day, he walks out with his mother in tow.

It feels as though the entire building gives a shudder of relief when the door closes behind them. But that might just be me.

He is back in the morning and this time he is in before me, which is a first. When I say he is in, I mean we assume he is in, because his car is parked outside. But, neither I nor anyone else see anything of him all day. I don't even know if his mother is also with him and I don't dare poke my head into his office to find out.

I'm not sure what he's trying to prove, if anything. Or what he is doing while in his office, other than sulking. But if this is how it's going to be while we wait for the outcome of the police investigation, the results can't come fast enough.

Fiona and Phil had arrived at the same time as me and are giving Trish a lift this week while her car is in the garage. She greets me and is considerably more relaxed than yesterday.

Phil sets up my laptop with all the business software it needs, and I feel better knowing no one is able to track me as I work.

I'm due at the building site for my usual Thursday afternoon and Fiona says she'll come with me. Mortifyingly, we have to call in to the police station on the way so I can fulfil my bail obligations and sign in. Fiona doesn't make any comment when I return to the car afterwards, thankfully, as I find the whole process demeaning. Anyway, we're glad of the opportunity to escape for a while and I'm pleased to get some work done.

We have the confirmation from Phil that Rex has spent the day in his office later, because he walked out again at five. This time alone.

15: Downfall of the King

Unannounced, DS Barker walks into the reception area at two o'clock on Friday. This time, he is with an older man. I see them arrive from my office.

'Ms Fraser, this is Detective Inspector Pattison.' My surprise must show on my face because he provides further explanation. 'He is now involved because this case has become more complex.'

'It has?'

Pattison stares at me intently, his brow furrowed. 'I'm not convinced, Ms Fraser, you've told us everything you should have done.' My stomach contents turn to acid.

'Have I not? I'm sure I did…' I try not to come across as flustered.

'Hmm. We'll see. We've come to discuss the initial findings. Is Mr Marchant in?'

'He is. I'll show you straight through.'

'At last!' Rex says, and he throws his arms in the air as he rises to meet the officers. 'It's about bloody time. I want that witch locked up.' He waves his hand in my direction, then presumably when it appears as if I might be about to leave, he says, 'No, you stay here.' But he is wrong. I'm going nowhere. Miss what is about to play out? Not a chance.

Barker introduces Pattison, then Rex returns to his seat behind the desk and leaves the rest of us standing. I offer the seats in front of the desk to the detectives while I retrieve a chair from the corner for myself. Pattison and Barker shuffle themselves around until they have everyone in view.

'This is an unusual case, so bear with us while we refer to our notebooks, won't you?' At that, Pattison delves into his jacket pocket and withdraws his pad as Barker does the same.

'We're also going to record the conversation, if it's all right with you?' Rex waves dismissively, his impatience plain to see.

'Just get on with confirming she's taken my money and get her out of here.' Rex, tired and frustrated, points repeatedly at me as he says this.

'I think I'd better explain what we've discovered first,' says Pattison.

Rex lets out a sigh of frustration and settles back, raising one ankle to rest across his other knee.

Unperturbed, Pattison continues, 'As you're aware, no one recognised the details of the account the two hundred and fifty thousand pounds was sent to. It doesn't match any of the known accounts for either suspect. Barker here, as an FI—'

'What's an FI?' Rex's tolerance levels are low.

'Financial Investigator. He is accredit—'

'Whatever. Get on with it.'

I'm embarrassed by Rex's churlish behaviour, and Pattison does well not to raise his eyebrows as he perseveres. 'Barker has made further enquiries with your bank and has discovered the recipient to be an offshore account.'

'An offshore account?' Rex glares at me in disbelief. 'I wouldn't have believed you capable, but here's the proof. You can't deny it now.' He turns to the officers. 'How do I get my money back?'

Pattison raises his hand. 'You misunderstand. The account is not in Ms Fraser's name, Mr Marchant. It's in yours.'

There is silence. Total and utter silence. Then…

The explosion.

'What! I don't have a fucking offshore account!'

Everyone in the building must have heard it. Pattison's voice is mellow by comparison.

'We have proof you do. And that the money was paid into it.'

Rex leans forward. His elbows on the desk. I can see him trying to work it out, his scrambled brain ticking away behind eyes too narrow-set to be trustworthy. He repeats, as though doubting himself, 'But I don't have an offshore account.'

In an effort to be helpful, I add to the conversation, 'I think maybe Rex has forgotten he opened it. I'm only saying that because I know if you have an offshore account, you have to declare it to HM Revenue and Customs and, because I have to deal with all the tax filings through the accountant, I know Rex has never done so.'

'As it was opened months ago, if he hasn't declared it, then he could already be in breach of the tax laws,' says Pattison, which is exactly the conclusion I want him to reach. I tilt my head in agreement, not feeling any further words are necessary.

Rex is still keen on arguing the point. 'That's irrelevant because I don't have an offshore account.' He sounds so certain.

'Even though your bank says you do?' Barker passes a piece of paper across the desk for Rex to read while I crane my neck in an attempt to see it, too.

Rex focuses on the details for mere seconds before desperation takes over. 'Even if it is my account, I haven't transferred any money into it.' Pattison stares at him for a few agonising moments.

'You're now admitting it is your account?'

'No, I'm not. I'm just saying. I didn't transfer any money anywhere. It's not something I do.'

Barker takes over. 'No. Not generally, perhaps. But you do have the capability to, and on Monday the thirteenth of April, the bank and your computer records tally. They show clearly you logged in to the bank, using your login, it's been confirmed on your computer, and made a transfer of fifty thousand pounds.' Rex's mouth drops open. Barker glances back at another sheet of paper he has withdrawn from his pocket. 'You also scheduled a further four payments for the same amount to be made on the following four days.'

'But I didn't.' Disbelief is gouged through every word. He then straightens in his chair. 'I wasn't even in the office that day. I went on holiday.' The ripple of relief that runs through him when he believes he's saved himself is almost visible.

'It's true,' I say. 'You did go on holiday that day, but you didn't leave until three o'clock, remember?' I look over at the officers. 'Are those transactions time-stamped by any chance?'

As luck would have it, they are, and timed well before Rex left the office. His eyes dart about the room as though searching for answers. 'Well, no, but I wasn't in the office all the time, was I? I went over to The Lodge. Remember?' He nods at me eagerly, seeking confirmation. As if I'm about to help him clear his name.

'I don't remember, sorry. I must have been busy with my work. But I assume the CCTV can confirm it?' I check back with the officers. 'One of the CCTV cameras shows the front of The Lodge, so it will have recorded anyone coming or going.'

Barker checks his notepad. 'The CCTV has been checked and there is no evidence of Mr Marchant entering The Lodge at any time on the day in question.'

Rex is baffled, and I can see the confusion plain on his furrowed brow. 'But I was with Phil and we met Eddie. They can vouch for me being there.' Barker nods and makes a note on his pad. My stomach churns over.

Rex holds his hands up as though he's had enough. 'Look. The point is, none of it matters anyway, because it's my company. Whether I do or don't have an offshore account that I supposedly transferred money into is utter bollocks because I'm the only shareholder and I can do whatever I want with the money in it because the buck stops with me.' I experience a lightening in my limbs at this statement. Adrenaline floods my veins because this is it, finally, the moment I have worked towards and waited for.

Pattison slides a piece of paper across the table. Rex stares at it.

It's from Companies House. The confirmation came in the post while Rex was away. And I know he is about to lose it. He picks it up, looks closer. I don't crane my neck this time. I know what it says. He glances over at me, then back at the paper, disbelief in every movement. I like that the detectives leave space for him to work it out.

'What have you done?' His voice is strained with emotion.

'With what?' I ask, nothing but innocence in mine, and I lean forward, confusion across my brow, as if I'm not sure what he's talking about.

'My company. The shares. They're in your name.'

'Oh!' My eyes widen in surprise. 'Well you did say you were going to transfer the company to me. Don't you remember?'

'Of course I don't remember. I never agreed to this.'

'You signed the Stock Transfer form, Rex. You told me you'd register it with HMRC and make the relevant changes at Companies House. In recognition of my years of dutiful service with the company, I think that's what you said.' He exhales loudly but I carry on. 'You told me you weren't happy working here. It had been a mistake to take it on after your father died and deep down you knew this was what your father would have wanted. I had no idea how quickly it would happen, though. And, I have to admit, I wasn't sure you'd go through with it at all.' He shakes his head as though trying to wake from a bad dream. 'I think I kept a copy somewhere if you want to see it, check on the signature.'

'What relevant changes at Companies House?' He is so tense he can barely speak.

'Terminating you as director and appointing me, of course.'

He jumps to his feet, exploding with rage.

'What?' His voice is pitched at a near scream. For a moment, I envisage him launching himself across the desk at me, as do Pattison and Barker as they quickly stand and raise their hands in an attempt to calm him.

'I wouldn't hand you my fucking company. It's mine! Why would I do that?'

'You did it to relieve yourself of the responsibility, that's what you said. But perhaps you had second thoughts?' Fury suffuses his face as he slams his fists on his desk.

'Second thoughts?' No longer aware of what he's saying, I move in for the kill.

'And decided to take some money with you. Which of course, being as this is now my company, is my money, so is in fact fraud.' I spread my hands wide towards the detectives. 'But I don't know. What's your take on it?'

Rex stares at the sheet again, aghast. 'I don't fucking believe this. You can't believe it, surely?' He waves it in desperation at the detectives.

Pattison draws the paper out of his hands. 'Seems obvious to me, Mr Marchant. I think you need to be aware that as well as logging in to your bank account, it's clear you also logged in to Companies House. You submitted the relevant forms to terminate your position as director and appoint Ms Fraser. You emailed the signed stock transfer form to HMRC. All your actions are captured on your computer and with your sign-ins.'

Rex's hand shakes as he gesticulates towards me. 'But she could have done all of that. She could have logged in to my computer and done it all.'

I pity him. 'You know as well as I do, Rex, how impossible it would be for me to carry out all those tasks. Since you brought in the new computer system, we all have our own unique logins, as we do with the bank. And, the first rule written in our company policies is not to share passwords. How could I have got into your computer or the bank without your login details?'

Pattison turns back to Rex and raises one eyebrow in question. 'Is this true?'

'Well, yes… but it wouldn't stop her.'

'Have you shared your passwords with her?' He has, because he's inherently lazy and will allow me to do any amount of his work. But he'll not admit it to the police because he'll lose any credibility by saying he's done so. It's also irrelevant whether he has or not anyway, because I know where he keeps them.

'No, but she's a conniving, devious c—'

'That is enough!' Barker raises his hand to emphasise words that don't need it.

All colour drains from Rex's face as he turns to me. 'You've swindled me out of my company.'

I am calm in my response. 'Be careful what you say, Rex. You don't want to be adding slander to the list of charges coming your way, do you?'

I can imagine the turmoil in Rex's mind. I know what he is experiencing because I have lived through enough of it over the last months and years. The desperate reach into the back of your mind to try to retrieve memories of conversations and deeds. Second-guessing. Triple-guessing. Wondering if you're going mad. Rex is only at the start of his journey into grappling with what has happened, and I know he faces a difficult time ahead. His chair breaks his fall as he slumps back a much-defeated man, his eyes staring somewhere into the distance.

Barker turns to me. 'You should have told me about this earlier.' And he raises the stock transfer form.

'I never imagined he would stick by his word.'

Pattison adjusts his position, clears his throat, and checks the notebook he holds in his hand. 'We do have more, which might clarify the situation.'

'I hope it clarifies the fact that bitch is insane and has stolen my company.' Rex sounds weary, and I'm not sure how much fight he has left in him for what is to come.

Pattison tilts his head in a noncommittal gesture. 'There are various parts of your search history which make for interesting reading. Barker?' And he encourages his partner to continue.

Barker reads from his own notebook, 'There have been further initial findings on your computer. We found searches into how to open an offshore account recorded months ago. More recently you searched for which countries didn't have an extradition treaty with the UK.' Rex's jaw drops and for a moment his mouth flaps open and shut like a gasping carp as if he's trying to say something but can't find the words. Unsurprisingly. 'Shortly after we found you'd renewed your passport.'

I jump in here. 'He asked me to take care of it for him. He does like his holidays.' Rex says nothing to deny this. He can't, the proof is only too easy to find.

Barker checks his pad again. 'You decided on Northern Cyprus—'

'For what?'

'For the place you were planning to run to. Knowing once the fraud was uncovered, we'd have no way of getting you back as there is no extradition treaty with Northern Cyprus.'

'No, this came up before with the other officers. It's all nonsense.' Rex holds his hands out towards the officers, his palms uppermost. 'Seriously, you think I'd put myself through all this for a lousy quarter of a mill?'

The expressions on both of the detectives' faces tell me as, along with the PCs, neither considers the sum of money "lousy", and they don't appreciate those who do either. I sense Rex's panic as he blunders on.

'Anyway, I wouldn't know how to open an offshore account and know even less about extradition treaties.'

'Obviously,' says Barker, 'Which is why you researched them.'

'But I didn't. That's what I'm telling you.'

'Are you sure?' says Pattison. 'Because you had flights booked out of Heathrow to Istanbul then on to Ercon Airport in Nicosia?'

'I didn't!'

'Believe me, Mr Marchant,' says Barker, 'You did. You booked the flights on the day you started taking the money. There's more besides. Our computer analyst tells me you've been spying on others in this company.' He raises his hand as Rex goes to speak. 'And don't tell me it's your company and you can do what you like. There are such things as privacy laws and you appear to have broken every single one of them.'

Rex leaps to his feet. 'So far, all you've told us about is all the stuff found on my computer. What about hers, eh? What does hers reveal?' Interesting, he's not denied the spying allegations, but is now keen to change the focus onto me.

'I'm coming to that.'

Rex's expression becomes one of smugness. I almost feel sorry for him. Almost.

Barker takes a deep breath and turns to me. 'These are only the initial findings and a complete forensic examination of the computers to provide a full evidential report could take months. But it does appear Rex was receiving copies of every email you received or sent.' I ensure I appear suitably shocked as I glance between Rex and the officers.

'Ah, it makes sense now,' I say, and explain about the email that arrived in my inbox from Rex's soon after he left. Then I turn to Rex. 'I can't believe you've done this. It's such an invasion of privacy. After everything I've done to keep the business going.' His mouth opens, about to retaliate, but Pattison has more to say.

'Mr Marchant. Your computer also reveals you have been receiving video footage streamed from various places within this building. What do you have to say about that?'

'No comment.' Rex finally recognises the trouble he might be in and clams up. I know he'll ask for his solicitor soon, or perhaps his mother.

'Did you know about this?' Pattison asks me.

'No, but I had my suspicions. Can you come with me for a moment? I have something to show you.' Pattison instructs Barker to remain with Rex and, for the benefit of the recording, says we are leaving the room. I take him to the cleaner's cupboard, unlock it, and retrieve the bin of air fresheners from the corner. His eyebrows rise when I remove the tarpaulin, but we return to Rex's office before I say anything further.

Rex puts his head in his hands and groans when we walk back in and he spots what Pattison is carrying.

Once seated again, Pattison says, 'Ms Fraser, can you tell me what we have retrieved from the cleaner's cupboard and why it was there?'

'Yes. This is my bin into which I recently collected all the air fresheners placed around the office. Six of them in total. The only room which didn't contain one was Rex's office.'

'Why did you collect them?'

'I had my suspicions we were maybe being spied on when I heard a colleague mention Rex had suggested ideas that were things that he himself had been researching, or had spoken to someone else in the office about. I wasn't sure how he was doing it, but then I remembered a conversation I'd had in passing with the cleaners one night. I'd thanked them for the new air fresheners and they said they had nothing to do with it, but it had been Mr Marchant who replaced them, and he'd been the one who put them in.' I shake my head. 'This was so out of character for him it should have raised an alarm bell with me at the time, but I was busy and with one thing and another, I didn't think of it again.'

'Until last week.'

'Indeed, I think it was me remembering them saying he'd put them in initially at the same time as the computer equipment being installed, which made me suspicious. I haven't checked them since though. I've not had the time, so I've no idea if they have cameras in them or not.'

'We'll take them to be checked out. But the most recent images received onto Rex's computer certainly tally with these objects having been moved into the bin and locked away.'

Barker gets to his feet and walks round to the other side of the desk. 'Mr Marchant, although other charges are likely to follow, you remain under arrest on suspicion of fraud and will now be taken into custody to face further questioning. Please stand.' When Rex does, too stunned to do or say anything further, Barker pulls out a pair of handcuffs, brings Rex's hands in front and places them around his wrists. Anger emanates from Rex's every pore as Barker places a hand on his shoulder and pushes.

Pattison walks out first, with Rex positioned between the two officers. I follow them, hardly daring to believe what I've got away with and trying my hardest to appear duly concerned about the turn of events. Every head turns to watch our progress and this final humiliation sparks further protest in Rex as he slows his pace then plants his legs wide and twists to glare back at me.

'Don't think you'll get away with this, you fucking bitch.'

'Be quiet,' Barker orders through gritted teeth as he pushes him harder, then harder still as Rex fights against him, struggling as Barker forces him to move again. I follow them outside, along with the rest of the staff who crowd out of the main door behind me. We gather in a throng as though about to wave off a happy couple after a wedding. Barker opens the rear door of the car, places his hand on Rex's head and tells him to mind it as he gets him into the back seat. We remain in place as he is driven away.

I check my watch and turn to the assembled staff, who are stunned into silence by the turn of events. 'There will be a meeting in The Lodge in half an hour, where I will update you all on what's happened. For now, I need to call Eddie and have a strong cup of tea. Who else wants one?'

Like a rerun of the "before work" meeting held earlier in the week, as the builders return from their various sites, Eddie asks them to wait in The Lodge. I walk over with the office staff.

I stand near Eddie, amazed at the strength I draw from him being next to me.

He leans over. 'You were most mysterious on the phone.'

'I was still trying to get my head around it all.'

'Intriguing.' His eyes widen, and I smile as I turn to the room.

'Could I have your attention for a minute, please?' Hush descends. 'The police returned this afternoon with their initial findings. I'm sorry to have to inform you it now appears Rex is responsible for taking the money out of the account last week.' I pause to let it sink in. 'I won't go into all the details because it's taken over two hours to go through it all with the police. Suffice to say it appears there is enough proof for them to take Rex back into custody.'

'He's going to be charged with stealing his own money?' Dean again.

'Not exactly. He's been arrested on suspicion of fraud. Apparently, other charges are likely to follow.'

'What charges?'

'I'm not sure. But I dare say we'll know more in due course.'

'Why is it fraud if it's his own company?' Dean is certainly persistent, and I'm not sure if it is because he is genuinely curious or one hundred per cent Team Rex. In which case, what I have to say next may not go down well.

'That's the other thing I need to tell you, which I hope doesn't disappoint too many of you.' My mouth dries and, as though made of jelly, my knees weaken because I don't know how they will take what I say next. 'This may come as a surprise to you. It did to me, but before Rex left last week, he transferred his directorship and one hundred per cent of the shares in the company to me. I now own Marchant & Son.'

The room erupts with cheers and clapping as Eddie vigorously shakes my hand, which is at once formal and, being the first time we have ever touched each other, weirdly thrilling.

'Congratulations.' His grin is broad enough to show his dimples. The reaction in the room shows I didn't need to have worried about telling them that part, after all.

We're not out of the woods, of course. The company, I mean. I will be reverting to Mr Marchant Senior's "We". The accounts are currently short by a quarter of a million, which will have to be replaced. I know the police investigations will continue for some time and who knows what they could yet reveal? And I don't expect Rex to go quietly either. Although I am hoping he will eventually see the money as recompense, as he does seem the sort of man who will leap at a short-term yield rather than want to work at anything for a long-term gain. But you never know. A court battle could be in my and the company's futures. If I haven't done my job properly, of course, and have inadvertently left him with a legal leg to fight on.

As it is, I suspect the charge of fraud will fail, anyway. There's a fine line between when the money was transferred and when the company officially became mine. Once investigated thoroughly, it will probably show at least some of the money was taken while Rex was still the director. I've already decided I will be magnanimous and drop the charge at the appropriate moment. If I let him keep the money, with a bit of luck he will end that particular fight because he is going to have several other charges to face: driving while uninsured, driving while under the influence of alcohol, not registering his offshore account with HMRC, workplace privacy issues, plus I dare say the police will suggest several others.

For the moment, though, as I look round the room, I know we could do with a celebration of some sort. An early summer party, perhaps? I will have to put my thinking cap on for a fitting way in which to mark this start of a new era.

'Can I have a quick word?' I say to Eddie, and we walk out of The Lodge to find some quiet.

'How can I help?'

'I think we should change the locks on both buildings. I know it's a hassle, but I'd feel better in my mind if I knew he couldn't get in. Sorry to land this on you.'

'It's no problem and makes perfect sense. I'll get two guys now and we'll do it before we finish this evening. Don't worry if you need to get off, I can let myself in.'

'No, no. I'll be there. I'm not one to make others work when I'm not.' He raises his eyebrows at me before going to make the necessary arrangements.

I then pull Phil to one side. 'I'm not sure if you are the person who can do this, Phil, or if you know of someone for me to approach, but we need to get the office and The Lodge swept for hidden bugs or cameras. I also want all the computer equipment checked over to ensure there are no trackers and everything is as it should be.'

'It's not something I can do, but I know of a company who can.'

'Excellent. We'll call them on Monday. The police have told me they'll be keeping Rex's and my computers for months, so I'm going to order a new one over the weekend. Perhaps you can help me set it up?' I ask in all hopefulness because getting the online back-up onto new equipment makes me nervous.

'Of course. I'd be delighted to.' While I think, *it takes all sorts*, he smiles before joining Fiona as she walks out of The Lodge.

'Are you okay?' she asks, placing her hand on my shoulder.

'Do you know what? I'm fine. He's in police custody and I feel as though a weight has lifted from my shoulders.'

Fiona leans in. 'I don't know how you managed it all, but well done.'

'I don't know what you mean,' I say, and grin at her. Rolling her eyes in disbelief, she announces she's had more than enough excitement for one week and is going to finish off what work she has to and leave for the weekend.

'I'll be in before you go,' I say, before turning my attention back to The Lodge as I have plenty of goodbyes to make yet.

A short while later, I leave to return to the office building, passing Eddie who is already overseeing the locks being changed on The Lodge.

'Nearly done here, then we'll be over with you,' he says.

'Excellent, thanks. I'll see you soon.'

There is a lightness in my step as I cross the yard. I can't stop the smile on my face. The relief at protecting this place, these jobs, along with my own, is overwhelming.

For the first time in forever I can look forward to the future, and a tingle of excitement runs through me at the prospect of reinstating all of Mr Marchant Senior's ideas and plans.

I run up the stairs of the office block and enter reception with more energy than I've possessed in a while.

Then stop.

The wind sucked out of my sails.

By Abigail.

16: A Mother Scorned…

Of course he's sent his mother.

She turns at my entrance.

Sharp suit. Blood red.

Every inch a tigress come to protect her cub.

My chest tightens, breaths quickening in response.

Trish's hand pauses, and she puts down the phone. Her warning call to me is too late. But it is fine. This confrontation was always going to happen. It is time to rip off the plaster.

'Mrs Marchant, it's good to see you.' I am cautious in my welcome as I don't know what, if anything, she knows.

'Don't give me that. Is it true?'

'Is what true?'

'I've spoken to Rex.'

'Right.' I give nothing away. 'Shall we go to my office?' I indicate towards the openness of the area, the presence of others she may not want to overhear what is about to pass between us.

'No. I have nothing to hide. Do you?'

'No.' It's difficult to read what's going on behind the frozen mask, but there is a tightness around her flinty eyes, a rigidity in her frame of barely suppressed anger.

'He tells me you've stolen the company from us.'

'It was never "us", it was only ever his, and I've done no such thing. He transferred it to me.'

'He'd never do that.'

'Wouldn't he?'

She blinks. 'He loves this company.'

'He hates it. He always has done. Ever since you forced him into taking up what you saw as his rightful place.'

'It *was* his rightful place. I didn't have to force him.'

'If he'd been interested in the business, then I'd agree. But he wasn't. And yes, you did force him.'

'I did no—'

'You insisted, Abigail. At a time when he was vulnerable and with few options before him. You placed him in a position of authority he was ill-prepared for, and you left him to it.'

'I have always supported him.'

'You were too idle to be what he needed. If you had wanted him to be successful with the business, you should have been prepared to take your place in it. Been a shareholder. Done some work. But you didn't want that, did you? You wanted the money, and that was all.'

'How dare you!'

'The truth hurts, doesn't it, Abigail. Because of your manipulation, Rex has wasted years of his life damaging a business his father built.'

'Oh, of course, you would bring it back to his father.'

'What do you mean by that?'

'Mr Bloody Perfect in your eyes. Don't think I don't know you were in love with him. It used to make me sick coming in here. You fawning over his every word. Yes, Mr Marchant. No, Mr Marchant.'

'I didn't fawn. I respected him.'

'Course you did.' I don't appreciate the sneer with which she says these words. And I don't want to continue in this direction. But she isn't letting me off that easily. 'I know you were fucking him.'

The obscenity makes me flinch. Like mother, like son. She's never accused me directly before, but it's what I've always suspected she thought.

'I was not.' It sounds lame as a response, but what else can I say?

'I don't believe you.' I hate the unfairness of her thinking something which isn't true.

'Believe whatever you want. The truth is, I respected the work he put in to make Marchant's a success. All Rex has done is destroy his legacy and risk losing the company and everyone's job. He's even stolen money, which will only further weaken the business.' She draws back. He clearly hasn't told her that part.

'He wouldn't.'

'He has. Ask the police.' Her shoulders sag; some of the fight gone out of her, but she's not done yet.

'He told me you had put the paperwork together and submitted it.'

'You shouldn't believe everything he tells you. His signature is on everything. How would I have done that? He's trying to shift the blame for his decision to hand over a company he was damaging. And I appreciate him doing so because at least he's finally seen sense and handed over what he could not control.'

'And you think you're the one to save Marchant's?'

'I know I am.' Silence follows, and I refuse to be the first to break eye contact.

She takes a step closer and her voice lowers, the threat in her tone hard to miss. 'This is not over, Alice. I will not let you destroy my son. I will find out the truth. I will sue you. And you will lose.' She marches past me to the door, bashing into my shoulder as she does so.

Shaken, I take a deep breath, and it shudders back out again. Thank God that is over.

Fiona rushes across from her desk to check on me as I collapse onto the sofa. Trish brings me water.

'Sorry, I didn't have time to call,' she says. I wave away her apology.

'It's fine. I knew I'd have to face her at some point. At least it's over with now.'

'That was tough,' says Fiona. She isn't wrong. It is going to take a while to recover from and I know I said things I shouldn't have, but once Abigail accused me, I couldn't stop myself.

Eddie walks in a few minutes later. He eyes me with concern. 'I just saw Abigail leave. Are you all right?'

'I'm okay. We exchanged a few words, that's all. It's done with now. Our views have been aired and we can move on.'

Unconvinced, he goes to change the locks while we finish up for the weekend.

I can't wait to get home, as I've had enough drama for one day. Opening a bottle of wine, I toast myself and tell George everything as I need to offload before the details haunt my night.

17: Topsoil

I wake to sunlight streaming through the window. The relief I experienced after such an intense period means I slept solidly for the first time in longer than I can remember. Although the bottle of wine might have had something to do with it, too.

I have a slow start to the day and enjoy pottering about with the spring sunshine pouring through the windows to brighten my cottage, the back door open, as I prepare for Dora coming round later. When I go to hang out the washing, there is a light breeze, the sun warm on my back. We can have coffee and cake in my south-facing front garden, as long as Dora is keen. I don't use the table and chairs out there nearly enough, and it will be good for her to have this gentle exposure to the village. A few people might pass the time of day with us, but there won't be many, and it will be better than her having to face a lot of people all at once at a village function.

Eddie said he was going to come round late morning or early afternoon, depending on when he can get the topsoil. The weather is settled and I'm looking forward to a lovely afternoon together in the garden. My thoughts drift to how I've felt in his presence recently and my growing feelings that I'm not sure how to communicate.

Dora arrives promptly at ten. She's brought homemade flapjack, and I'm pleased to see she's baking again. She's also perfectly happy with my idea to sit outside, so after I've closed the back door, I carry the tray of coffee and flapjack while she goes ahead to open the front door for me. We both sit for a moment, eyes closed as we enjoy the sun warming our skin. It has been a long winter. Tulips have replaced the daffodils on the verges and I have a variety of bulbs flowering which vie for attention and provide plenty of colour at this time of year. With all that has been going on recently, though, I've not taken a moment to pause and take in what has been growing out here at all, and some are already going over.

'How's your week been then? Any news from Esme?'

'It's been marvellous. We've spoken again, and she's planning to come to visit on the May bank holiday weekend, the first one.'

'Fabulous news. How will it work? Is she going to stay with you?'

'Oh, no. I think it might be too soon.' I agree, but didn't want to say. 'She's going to stay at the hotel, the one outside town. Do you know where I mean? I can't think of the name, but it's in that chain.'

'Yes, I know. It makes sense for you to meet somewhere neutral first and go from there.'

'I was thinking of the garden centre. You can have a wander there and a bit of something to eat.' She places her hand on her stomach. 'I'm nervous already.'

'Of course you are. It's understandable.'

'I've been keeping busy to distract myself. I even,' and she glances across at me to see what my reaction will be, 'went to the coffee morning.'

My smile tells her all she needs to know. 'Well done.' It's wonderful she's getting out and about again.

'Which reminds me, have you seen Maisie Brooks' cottage is now rented out?' I haven't, even though I've driven right past it more than once.

'It'll be a relief for her. She must be struggling with her parents and trying to keep the cottage going, too. Have you heard who's moved in?'

'She's a single woman, that's all I know. But I've seen Olivia again. Bless her, she dropped by with some chocolates and stopped for a cup of tea, and she and Kyle are delighted to have someone living there. She's terribly friendly, apparently. Came round with some flowers for Olivia to introduce herself.'

'That's good to hear. So many people move in nowadays and keep themselves to themselves.'

'Not this one. She's been buying drinks at the pub and chatting with everyone. She was the talk of the coffee morning, as you can imagine.'

'Let's hope she throws herself fully into village life, then. We could do with some fresh blood around here.'

'Indeed. Anyway, how about you? How's your week been? Things any better at work?' I hear my phone ring inside and rise from my seat.

'It's been an eventful week and I'll fill you in shortly, but I'd best go and see who that is.' I retrieve my phone from the kitchen worktop. It's Barker.

'Good morning, Ms Fraser. Sorry to call on a Saturday, but I wanted to update you on the situation.'

'Of course, it's no problem. I hope everything's all right?'

'It is, but I wanted you to be aware we released Rex Marchant on bail this morning. There was no reason to keep him any longer.'

'Oh. Okay. Thanks for letting me know.' My stomach churns as though snakes roil inside.

'We've warned him to keep his distance, but I wanted you to know he was out.'

'Thank you, but I can't help wishing he'd increase the distance by leaving the country.'

'Not possible, I'm afraid, bail conditions. He won't be going anywhere.' Shame. It is bumping into him around here that will keep me awake at night. Him showing up at the office and causing a scene that will keep me looking over my shoulder.

'Thanks for letting me know.' We end the call, but my high spirits have evaporated, disappearing into the ether like steam from a kettle. Nausea twists at my stomach as thoughts of work on Monday fill me with dread, yet again. With the locks changed, he can't get in, but he is bound to appear during the working day. It would be the sort of contrary thing for him to do, when he didn't care a jot about being there when it was his company. Having already had the confrontation with Abigail I also have no appetite for another, and am seriously starting to consider whether what I've done has been worth it.

I go back outside, leaving the front door ajar.

'It was the police. There have been some developments.' And I go on to give her the highlights of what has occurred during my week.

'Crikey. But now you're in charge, it's got to make life easier for you, hasn't it?'

'Yes, in some ways, but Abigail's already had a go at me, and I'm feeling sick about it all again because the police have just told me they've let Rex out on bail. The thought of facing him anytime soon is not an appealing one.'

'He's not going to approach you though, is he? He'll be in more trouble if he does.'

'I'm not sure he'll think of it that way—' My hand leaps to my chest as the front door slams behind me. 'Damn.' Dora doesn't react at all, which shows exactly who is the more highly strung of the two of us.

'Oh, are you locked out? I've got a spare remember, don't worry.'

'Thanks. But the back door's unlocked. It made me jump, that's all. Do you want another coffee?'

'No thanks, help yourself to the flapjack.'

'I will do. Yours are delicious. I overbake mine.'

'Ah, you know what the trick is?'

'No.'

'Don't cook them for as long,' she laughs, which is good to hear as I take my first mouthful and nod at her wisdom. She then slaps the table. 'I know what else I've been meaning to say to you. I was reminded, looking at your fridge, then it went clear out of my head again.'

'What?' I mumble through the flapjack.

'I've been invited to the wedding of the year too.' Her face lights up, along with mine.

'Brilliant. We can go together.'

'We can. Although I can't think why I've been invited. Not after, well… you know.' It is the first reference she's made to her incident at all.

'People aren't thinking about that, Dora. You've played a major role in this village for years. Of course they'd want you to be there.' Her cheeks colour as she smiles.

'I have to say it has given my confidence a real boost.'

'Good. What are you going to wear? I think I'll have to treat myself to something new.'

'Me too. I don't have anything fancy enough. We could go shopping together?'

'That's an excellent plan. We'll sort out a date in a few weeks' time. I have a bit on at the moment.'

A couple of locals have walked by as we sat there and said hello. Harry O'Connor from the stables drove past in Laura's horse lorry and waved out of the window. Otherwise, our chat was uninterrupted and Dora helps me with the front gate as I carry the tray out and through the side passage to the back garden. She then leaves me to go and make a call to Esme and I enter the kitchen. There's a weird smell when I walk in. I sniff but can't place it, so I open the back door again to freshen the room.

I wash up and put everything away, humming to myself as I do so. There is a good chance Eddie will arrive at any point from now on, but as I'm not sure exactly when he'll get here, I decide I'll make a call on putting lunch together when he does. I also remember I haven't bought him the drink I owe him yet, and mull over this as I peer in the fridge to check I have enough in if he does want feeding. Perhaps I should invite him out this evening? For the drink, I mean. Not like a date. Not that sort of invitation. I'm not sure what he'll make of it if I do. Do I want it to be a date? More importantly, will *he* think of it as a date? Or am I being presumptuous? Perhaps it will be better if we met one lunchtime for a casual drink at the pub instead? That feels more relaxed. But then is that telling him how I feel about him? Maybe an evening drink would be better? These contrary thoughts and more go through my mind as I potter around. I think about his home life as I get the washing in. I know he's been single for a while, although there was a woman he once brought along to the work Christmas party. But only the once. And it was a while ago. Folding the clothes on the kitchen table, I consider the conversations we've had and try to remember if he's mentioned a new partner at any point. Then smile as I become conscious of where my focus has been.

'Sorry, George. I hope you understand,' I say, as I lift the pile of clothes to take it to the airing cupboard upstairs.

'Who's George?'

I yelp, draw the washing that bit closer to me, and stop in my tracks as I enter the sitting room.

Rex is on my sofa.

A satisfied smile spreads across his face, but does not reach his eyes. He stands as I drop the clothes and rush for the front door, but he beats me to it, slamming his body between mine and it. My hand is on the lever handle, trapped behind his back and, as I try to push it down, he presses harder, and the pain that shoots through my hand makes me squeal. He is twenty plus years younger than me and I am no match for his strength.

'Don't bother trying.' His voice is little more than a whisper in my ear. He hasn't showered any time recently, body odour obvious up close. His breath is sour, the smell of alcohol on it only too apparent. I ease away from him then take a step back and, as he releases his pressure on the door and stands straight, he gestures with his head for me to go back into the sitting room then pushes me on the shoulder when I am already moving, causing me to stumble. I hear the catch go on the door to lock it. 'And don't start yelling or I'll silence you quicker than you can get the first word out.'

'What are you doing here?'

'What do you think?' His fury is obvious, the words spat out with venom, and only the most vigorous adjectives can be used to describe his level of agitation.

'You'll be in trouble with the police.'

'I'm already in trouble with the police. You've seen to that.'

'I don't know what you mean.'

'You know exactly what I mean.' He thrusts his chin towards me. 'I don't know how you did it but I'll find out.'

I crouch and gather the clothes, as though his presence doesn't bother me, putting them in a pile on a chair. But I shake as I do so. I debate whether to sit but as he doesn't, I remain standing and face him.

'What do you want?'

'The truth. How about you start with why you took my company from me?'

'I didn't. You gave i—' His palm whips across my face. Shock makes tears well as my hand rises to my cheek. My breath shudders in my chest as I gaze fearfully from beneath lowered lids. I swallow, trying to wet my dry mouth. 'You told me it's what your father would have wanted.'

'Oh, I know it's exactly what he'd have wanted. Shame, for you, he died before making it official.' He leans in closer to me. 'And I told you no such thing.' Ignoring this but intrigued by his first statement, I can't help but ask,

'What do you mean, you know it's what he'd have wanted?'

'As if you didn't know. All that fucking mentor stuff made me want to vomit. You were all he could ever go on about. His bloody protégé. That's what he called you. We'd have to listen to him drone on about how brilliantly you'd handled a client, or a contract, or whatever. It was like you walked on water and it

193

was sickening.' He pauses, his body rigid, fists flexing. 'He saw you as his successor. Not me.'

'I didn't know.' While we'd worked closely, he'd never given me any indication this was how he felt about me, and I could understand how it would have been annoying. It was out of character for Mr Marchant Senior, too. Thoughtless of him. Unless he was actively trying to irritate his family.

'I don't know how my mother stood it. It was so obvious you were having an affair.'

'We weren't.' I blurt out these words as forcefully as I can. As with Abigail, I don't mind being blamed for things I have done, but not for those I haven't.

'I don't believe you. And neither would my mother.'

'Believe what you want. I'm telling the truth.'

'You wouldn't know the truth if it bit you on the backside.'

'That's rich coming from you.' I pause. 'Why did you keep me on if you felt like this?'

'Because much as I hated having you around, you knew how it all worked, and he'd never bothered to teach me.'

'To be fair—' His hand strikes the other cheek this time. My head spins. As the dizziness fades, I open and close my jaw to test it before trying again. 'Didn't your mother ever tell you not to hit women?' He doesn't disappoint by giving me an answer.

But what he had said – "he'd never bothered to teach me" – causes a flame to flare deep inside. I hate injustice. Blame laid where it has no right being. And I've always been protective of his father. The unfairness of his words causes anger to bolt through my veins until like molten lava, it erupts. 'You never showed an ounce of interest in the business. You still don't. You only ever wanted the money. Just like your mother. And you're not prepared to do the work involved to get it.'

'I was never given the chance.' I see now with these words he'll never believe anything other than that he was hard done by. He's framed his reason for failure in the way which suits him and laid the blame for it firmly at his father's door. It is hardwired into him, his excuse, no doubt planted and encouraged by his besotted mother, and there is no point trying to convince him otherwise. He will never see any other point of view and I'll get nowhere trying to reach any kind of understanding and will have to find another way out of this situation.

'You know, I hated seeing you in the office every day knowing what you'd done with him.'

'You made that obvious, not that I *had* done anything with him.' He ignores the correction I make.

'What was this, then, you taking my company, revenge?'

'It was me saving the jobs and the business you seemed determined to destroy.' There, I've said it, an admission of sorts, the words out of my mouth before I had a chance to check them. For a fleeting moment, a horrible fear springs to mind that he's recording me. He has form. But then he wouldn't have hit me if he was.

'So you admit it? Wanted to play the hero, did you? Make everyone love you. Is that it?' He leans closer. 'I was sorting it. Some big deals were about to come in.' What nonsense. He lives in a fantasy world.

There's no point arguing with him on something we'll never agree about. I move on. 'What are you going to do?'

'I'm going to get you to tell the police the truth.'

'I've already done that and I won't be changing my statement.'

'We'll see.'

His sneer causes fear to slither down my spine as I glance at the back door, still open. I try to calculate if I can reach it in time. Even getting as far as the garden will increase my chance of escaping him, or getting someone's attention.

I've not been subtle, though. Without taking his eyes from me, he walks through the kitchen and closes the door, locks it and removes the key which he places in his jeans pocket. On his return, he takes a knife from the block on the side and reaches for a bottle of whisky from the shelf.

'Maybe this will help you change your mind.' He shows me the knife in his hand, as if I didn't see him pick it up. He's chosen the biggest one. Of course he has.

'What's your plan, Rex?' He may be many things, but I can't see him as some sadistic torturer who is about to put me through hell to get what he wants. He unscrews the lid and swigs straight from the bottle. Dutch courage? Or does he, in fact, have a drink problem? It's the first time I've considered the possibility.

I hear a vehicle draw to a stop outside and my stomach drops. Eddie. I don't want him to get involved in this. Rex peers out of the window.

'What's Lumbers doing here?'

'He's delivering topsoil.'

'Oh, yeah. Doing you a favour, is he? I bet it's come straight off a site.'

'Not your problem anymore, is it?' I'm not sure why I'm being combative, but I can't stop myself. He brings out the worst in me.

I can't see out of the window from where I stand, but hear a clank, which I picture as being Eddie taking his wheelbarrow off the topsoil. A further rattle and bang, I imagine, is him releasing the side of the truck to get easier access to the load. The sound of shovelfuls of soil filling the wheelbarrow is obvious to us both.

'Will he take it round the back or is he expecting to see you?' Uncertainty has crept into Rex's voice.

Before I can reply, the doorbell rings. I look at him. 'He knows I'm here and if I don't answer, he'll go to Dora next door and she's not long left, so she knows I'm here, too.' He has a decision to make. The doorbell rings again.

'Okay. Answer it and get rid of him.' I'm not sure it's going to be that easy.

I flick the lock off with a clunk and open the door. Eddie is turned half away, staring down the street. He spins back, a smile on his face. I keep mine deadpan. Squinting in the sunshine.

'Hiya, I've got the topsoil.' He indicates over his shoulder towards his truck. I can't have appeared less interested. But he doesn't notice and continues. 'Last week was fun so we could have lunch, then I'll get it unloaded.' I consider whether I can get out of the door before Rex can stop me, but he is behind it, keeping the opening narrow. The point of the knife is in my side, sweat causing a sting where it's already nicked me.

'I can't do lunch.' Eddie's enthusiasm is undiminished as he presses on.

'Oh, don't worry, you don't have to do a thing. I've brought it with me.'

'I meant I don't want to do lunch.' His smile falters and my heart twists with the pain I am causing.

'Oh, okay.' He takes a step back and ensuring Rex can't see the hand furthest away from him, I raise it in front of but close to my body, palm facing Eddie. I then bring my thumb across the palm and close my fingers over the top of it. 'I'll unload the soil then, shall I?' I don't think he's seen the hand gesture, so I make eye contact, then drop my line of sight to my hand.

'Don't bother, come back another time.' As I speak, I see him watch my hand, his face expressionless, and my heart sinks. It appears he has either been spinning me a line when he told me about all the police dramas he'd seen or he's forgotten something crucial from them that I need him to remember right now.

'I've already made a start unloading and as I'd set aside the day to get it done, I might as well get on with it. But don't you bother yourself.' His words sting. His irritation with me hurt to hear and I hate being so rude towards him. He turns away without another word and I close the door on him. I stand for a moment, my forehead pressed against the wood.

'I think he wants to get into your pants.'

'Don't be vulgar.'

'You're right. Even the thought of you two doing it is disgusting.'

I sigh and return to the sitting room, closely followed by Rex. This time I take a seat, as despair threatens to overwhelm me. What am I to do? Help is so close at hand. And yet so far. I hear the trundling of the wheelbarrow as Eddie pushes it through the passageway, and when I lean forward in my seat, I glimpse him continuing up to the top of the garden and tipping the soil into my vegetable beds.

Surely, he must realise something is wrong. After last week. When I couldn't have been more welcoming. We'd enjoyed lunch. We'd spent a relaxing time together as he'd made the vegetable beds. We'd got on well this week, too. Only last night he was more than happy to change the locks and I'd stayed back while they were done. He must be wondering what has gone wrong between us since to make me act as coldly to him as this? As things stand, I need him to call for help and it hasn't even occurred to him I'm in trouble.

Rex withdraws a pad and pen from his back pocket and hands them to me.

'What are these for?'

'They are for you to rewrite your statement. Tell them what really happened.'

I stare at him for a moment. 'I've already told you, I won't be doing that.'

'It's going to be a long night then,' he says, and takes another swig from the bottle. I allow myself the brief fantasy of him drinking the whole thing, then falling into an alcoholic stupor, and me walking out of here unscathed. But he is so wired I'm sure the alcohol entering his system will burn off without a chance of that happening, the disappointing reality causes the dream to thin and dissipate like smoke on a summer's day.

Sunshine pours through the window as I focus on the pad. Should I start writing something to appease him? Perhaps if I do, and he is happy with it, he will go. Yeah… right. Without the back door open, it's stifling in here. Sweat trickles between my breasts as I flap the collar of my top in an attempt to cool myself and I roll up my shirtsleeves. His twitching and jittering irritates me. It's too hot in here for all that movement.

There's the smell again. I sniff the air. It is familiar, yet out of place. Acrid. With both doors to the outside world closed, it is stronger in here. Thick. The start of a sickening headache between my eyes. I peer around the room, trying to see where it is coming from. Rex notices and stands to the side. I gasp as I spot the source at the far end of the sofa. He smiles. A can of petrol, the fumes released cloying in the enclosed space.

I glance back at Rex with alarm. He wouldn't? Surely? Now seated, he fixes his eyes on mine and I know he absolutely would.

I start writing, which is difficult because I don't want to write what I've done in case it falls into the wrong hands. Instead, I begin with my relationship with Rex and all the bad things he's brought into my world. It will buy me some time before I have to approach the meaty stuff.

He is on his feet again, pacing the room. So agitated he can't keep still. The knife hangs at his side, the bottle frequently to his lips. Each time he passes the window, he peers out to keep an eye on Eddie, but so he isn't spotted, he keeps back from the glass.

'Your mother must be worried about you.'

'Don't pretend to care about her.'

'I don't, particularly. But she must be. Does she know you're out?'

'Of course.'

'Does she know where you are?'

'No. I took the car and left.'

'Not stopping for even a shower.' He shrugs. 'She'll know you're here. She's probably told the police.' Wishful thinking.

'She'd never do that.' No, she'll protect her rotten son to the end. I am already aware. She'll let him get away with anything. Murder, even. I've never understood mothers who do that. Those who can't see the reality of what they've bred and defend them instead of pulling them into line. But then I'm not a mother, so what do I know?

I add a few more words to my pad, two of them; mummy's boy. When I run out of things to write about the son, I'll start on the mother.

From where I sit, I can't see Eddie out of the bay window, although I can hear him shovelling soil. Each time he trundles the wheelbarrow along the passage behind me, I draw comfort from him being so close. Then I glance out of the back door to watch him carry on up the garden.

Rex must have parked his car in the back lane somewhere, that's how he got in here. Perhaps it will be spotted by someone? Perhaps. But not unless it is being searched for. Or looks as though it has been abandoned. And it could be days before someone comes to that conclusion. My best bet is if he's parked illegally. That will be reported in hours.

As I consider what to write next, I see a car pull in further down the road and on the other side. Rex spins round at the fireplace and peers out at Eddie again.

'How long is he going to take?'

'I know he'd put aside the day so…' I hold my hands out and shrug. He focuses his attention back on me.

'Finished yet?'

'No.' And I quickly put pen back to paper.

I consider bashing him on the head each time he paces to the fireplace and has his back to me. He clearly isn't worried about me doing so. Probably doesn't think me capable. But whilst I am, I have mere seconds in which to act. And can't see anything within reach which will make an impact significant enough to immobilise him sufficiently and allow me to get out of the cottage. I can't make my move now, but I'll give it a damned good try if the opportunity arises.

He takes another gulp from the bottle, his movements unsteady as his hand drops back to his side. He cuts a pathetic figure, and unexpectedly, a wave of something I don't recognise sweeps through me. Guilt, maybe? Or is it sorrow for what I've done? I can't avoid the fact I've brought him to this point and for the first time, I consider whether I've gone too far. I was so driven and focused on the outcome, I didn't consider what I was doing to another human being. After everything, have I only lowered myself to his standards and become the abuser? I don't like the answer produced. Shame suffuses my face with heat as I bend over my pad. Maybe I can reverse my actions? At least most of them. Perhaps I can simply give him the company back? Maybe that would be the honourable thing to do. I look over at him and swallow before speaking. My words are croaky before I clear my throat.

'You know, we could come to an agreement. Maybe split the shares?' Unexpectedly, he laughs loudly.

'Are you trying to trick me? I'm not a fool. I know, you know.' And he waves the knife in my direction. 'You two were close. I know he'd have told you. He did, didn't he? Dad told you what he'd done?'

I shake my head. 'I don't know what you're talking about.'

'He must have told you. The papers. Mum found them. All neatly stacked in his safe.'

As confused as the alcohol loosened thoughts in Rex's head appear to be, I ask, 'Found what?'

'The coda… coda…'

Blood drains from my head. My voice is faint as I say, 'Codicil?'

'Yup, that's it.' He gesticulates with the knife in my direction again. 'All written up and signed it was, packaged with the transfer forms.' I can't believe what I suspect I'm about to hear.

'Lucky for me, he was dead before he got to lodge it with the will at his solicitor's.' He comes closer, points the knife in my direction again. 'Unlucky for you.' And he laughs.

I wait until his laughter fades away. I have no words.

He points the knife at me. 'Eighty.' Then at himself. 'Twenty.' The manic giggle that follows rankles, but all other emotions evaporate as fury rages through my veins. I've lived all these years with the sadness, knowledge and guilt Mr Marchant Senior had died thinking his love for me wasn't reciprocated because I didn't react when he touched me. It was, I just ran out of time to let him know. But he'd still shown his love by following through on the assurances he'd once made to me.

My next words are as cold as ice.

'What did you do?

He grins, widens his eyes, then placing a finger across his lips, whispers, 'As soon as he was dead, we burnt it all.'

As soon as he was dead…

'You found out *before* he died?' An icy shiver passes down my spine.

'Yup. Mum said she'd deal with it.' *Oh. No, no, no. She can't have.*

'Deal with what, Rex?'

'His insulin. She tampered with it.' He leans in as though about to impart a secret. 'She doesn't know I know, but I saw her.' He straightens, unsteady on his feet. 'I'm not saying it definitely caused what happened. Maybe it did. Maybe it didn't.' He shrugs as if it is just one of those things. Maybe his mother did kill his father. Maybe she didn't. His voice tapers off as he gazes out of the window. 'We'll never know.' I dare not move.

He turns.

His eyes meet mine.

And there is a moment.

A release in us both.

I can almost see the weight of the knowledge he's carried lift from his shoulders now the truth has spilled out. Simultaneously, my burden of guilt washes from my body as though it was an outer skin now sloughed by a monsoon under which I want to hold my arms outstretched with relief. Vindication. That's what this revelation is. Vindication for everything.

The bastard. He knows exactly what he's done. He and his bitch of a mother. They stole my future. My guilt is gone at having taken his. He'll get nothing from me.

Not now.

I fix him with a look fit to shatter glass. And he freezes.

Realisation swiftly follows.

At what he's revealed.

And to whom.

A shadow passes behind his eyes as a chill tightens my scalp.

Another slug of whisky passes his lips before he places the bottle on the floor and picks up the petrol can. I hear no sloshing so it is near full. He doesn't smoke. Will he have a lighter on him? Has he planned that far ahead? Apparently not, as he takes my matches from the mantelpiece and puts them in his top pocket.

I have to get out.

'How about something to eat?' I suggest, my voice betraying the turmoil inside.

'Not hungry.'

'Only thirsty?' I scathingly reply. 'I think you could do with some food to soak up the alcohol.'

'You're not my fucking mother. Shut up!' He shakes the petrol can in my direction. I draw back. The stink only intensifies. My head pounds. 'What are you going to do?' There is colour in his cheeks now. His eyes are glassy as the whisky takes effect.

'Torch the place. I have to now.' He clenches and unclenches his jaw. Goosebumps prickle across my skin. I can't think of a worse way to die.

'You may be many things, Rex. But I don't think you're a murderer.' He walks away, swings his arms – knife, fuel, knife, fuel. Turns and points the can at me.

'You know nothing about me.'

'I know plenty. You'll kill yourself too.'

'Like you care.'

'You haven't made it easy for me to care, Rex. But you're young. You can turn things around. But not if your next charge is for murder.'

'I'm facing so many already. What's it matter?'

'Don't be daft. The others are minor. A slapped wrist. A fine. With your fancy lawyers, you'll probably get to walk away. But not if you do this.'

He staggers. Rights himself. Puts the can on the chair in the bay window, in the full glare of the sun. I half rise as he retrieves his bottle and swigs.

'Rex, I don't think you should—'

'Shut up! Just shut up! Stop telling me what to fucking do!' He spins round, waving the bottle as he loses his balance and nearly falls.

I take a risk, place the pad and pen on the side table. 'Let me move the can.' I half rise again.

'Don't you go anywhere near it.'

'But, Rex—'

'But, Rex…' he mimics me. Whines better than I do. 'God, you make me sick with your nagging.' He points the knife at me. 'Take one step towards it and you're dead. Right?'

I nod and know I have to change tack. I place my hands with determination on my knees.

'Right. I'm going to get us something to eat. Yeah? I'm hungry. You must be too. We could be here for hours.' He pauses, his body unstable, worse as he lifts the bottle once more. Maybe he will pass out after all.

I rise carefully, receiving no objection, then edge out of the living room. Relieved to get a wall between me and the can. Rex follows. Eddie is up the garden, the wheelbarrow tipped over the edge of a sleeper as he shakes out its contents. I reach for the window catch to let in some air.

'Don't.' Rex climbs onto a stool at the breakfast bar. 'Drop the blind.' If I can't open the window, it is the next best thing.

Maybe Eddie will think me having the blind closed in the middle of the day is odd and take some action. Maybe…

I open the fridge and glance at Rex, who sits as though he is an invited guest I am happy to entertain. 'Sandwich? Sausage roll?' He waves at me with the knife.

'Whatever. Just get me some food.' Then I see what else he has. What he'd carried through from the other room. The pad. Damn. He starts reading as I try to distract him by emptying the contents of the fridge in front of him. Food is the last thing I need. But I grab the bread from the side. Rip open the bag and lay several slices on the worktop.

'I'm going to have to use a knife to butter these, Rex.' He, eyelids drooping, doesn't react as I slowly open the cutlery drawer, and I let him see me carefully lift a non-threatening variety from its tray. As the drawer swooshes shut, his gaze drops to the pad again. I grab fillings, ham, cheese, mustard, pickle, and slam them onto the bread in no particular order.

'Hey. This isn't what I told you to write. This is just a list of how mean Rex is, boo hoo,' he mimics me again. Badly. 'Where's that bloody pen…' He slips off the stool, nearly losing his balance. Heads to the sitting room. I open my mouth to stop him. Then close it again. Once he is out of sight, I grab the stool, lift it and, holding it by the legs, run at the back door, smashing the seat part against the glass in the top half with all my might. Wood splinters, glass shatters. But not enough to break through to the outside world. I swing the stool back to have another go. Hear a roar behind me. A whoosh as oxygen sucks from the air. A blood-curdling scream as Rex falls back into the kitchen. Flames leap up his body. His hair's alight as he hits the floor.

'Fuck!' I run to the cooker, rip the fire blanket from the wall and fall to my knees, throwing it onto a writhing Rex. Holding it tight to his body, I smother the flames as his body contorts beneath me and he screams. Toxic black smoke rolls through from next door as I hear splintering glass. My eyes sting, and I gasp for breath, coughs wrack my chest as I dash to the door, and orange red flames ravenously devour everything before me, my hand burnt as I pull it closed against the searing heat. Every second is needed. Rex hasn't moved but moans when, back on my knees, I struggle to lift his hips enough to slide my hand into his back pocket to retrieve the key.

'Come on, get up,' I attempt to yell, my hoarse voice breaking into a wracking cough.

Back door unlocked, I suck in the fresh air as I throw it wide then return to Rex. He moves, clothes smouldering, face blistered, as he tries to get to his feet. I go to help him, an arm around his waist, supporting his body as we get outside. Once clear of the cottage, he shoves me away. I fall, hitting the garden table before landing hard on the paving, as he staggers off up the garden. I rise, coughing, my breaths rasping in my aching chest as two police officers tackle him to the ground barely past the orchard.

Eddie runs out of the passage, ashen-faced. Relief swamps his features as he spots me and wraps me in his arms. Safe. I sob into his chest, hearing sirens in the distance.

Barker and Pattison appear with paramedics in tow. Taken to the top of the garden to be checked over and treated, Rex is attended to first and carried off on a stretcher.

I sit with an oxygen mask on my face. A paramedic treats my hand as I gaze at my cottage. Smoke billows out of the door. No flames though, which surprises me.

Eddie, by my side, notices. 'The fire's under control. I had an extinguisher in the truck. The fire crew will deal with the rest.'

I mumble, 'Thank you,' through the mask.

'I'm afraid it's going to be a mess.' He raises his eyebrows. 'But luckily you own a building firm.' My smile is weak.

'You raised the alarm, too.'

'Of course I did. That hand signal. Clever.' He nods his approval.

I pull the mask to the side. 'I don't know how to thank you.'

'Well, it might be two drinks you owe me now.' He grins as I laugh lightly before breaking into another violent bout of coughs. I reach for his hand with my good one.

'It's a date.'

Epilogue

Most people hate doing administration tasks. Given half the chance, they'll willingly let someone else do everything for them. This can be a perfect solution, if you trust that person. But when someone knows nothing, checks even less and signs whatever is put in front of them. When they trust those they shouldn't and then treat them like dirt. Well, then there can be a problem.

Eventually, the put-upon have had enough, and I certainly had.

Abigail made the mistake of not only being a horrible person but also keeping her distance. She would have been a far more worthy adversary than Rex. But instead of rolling up her sleeves and getting involved, her entitlement is such she preferred to play puppet master and manipulate Rex into doing her bidding so she could continue to live as she had before, but still without lifting one finger of her perfectly manicured hand. Her biggest error was in not becoming a shareholder. It would have been far harder for me to have got rid of them both.

Once Rex revealed what she had done, what part she had played in Mr Marchant Senior's death, I knew I would never forgive her. I swore there and then I would do all I could to bring her to justice.

As for Rex, there's one simple thing to say about him. He is a fool and he misjudged me. To him, I am someone to patronise, bully and gaslight. Someone he considers past it and only capable of jumping to his tune. To him, I am already an old lady of no particular interest or consequence, and absolutely no threat to him or his world. Meek, mild, and invisible little Alice. That's how he sees me. Someone to be used. But while invisibility is something which happens to older women, it can be used to our advantage, so underestimate us at your peril.

Big mistake, Rex. Huge.

Because I had something else on my side. Experience. And you can't buy that.

I'd moved out to the Costa del Sol with my family in the 1970s although was too young to realise we were there because at the time there was no extradition treaty with England and my family were, well, criminals. It was there, mingling with others in the criminal fraternity, that I met George. Our families were connected by their mutual interest in stealing stuff. George and I played together as children, went out as teenagers and married ridiculously young; barely adults.

I know I was naïve when I met George. I should have seen how precarious our future was likely to be when going out on a date depended on whether he'd won enough on the game machine in the pub to pay for it. He matured as time went on, but only by becoming more sophisticated in the games he played. Instead of being concerned by this, I found it intoxicating, our life together colourful and turbulent, and I'm sure I didn't know the half of what he was up to.

I learned over time that George was a grifter or con artist, and eventually I became his accomplice, or shill, to use the technical term. That makes us out to be horrible people and certainly on both sides of our family there were plenty of those. But George and I played things a different way. Despite the stock he came from, George had a strong moral compass, one which appealed to me. So while he'd learned his dubious skills from his family, he used them for good instead of evil. A tenant in trouble with their landlord? A restaurant unable to pay the hike in their protection fees? A company in the hands of the wrong person? George came to their rescue. Think of him more as a Robin Hood figure than a Dick Turpin. He carried out his fair share of small-time cons when the need arose but, when possible preferred an elaborate con, which required plenty of planning and preparation to achieve a satisfying outcome. That was where he excelled.

And these skills were what he taught me.

Planning. Preparation. Patience.

It was easier back then in many ways. A simpler time. A more innocent time. No internet. No mobiles. No checks and double-checks.

We were never going to be rich. But we could live with ourselves.

Of course, there was always the possibility we'd make enemies.

And in hindsight, working as we had chosen to, increased the risk of that.

George had his eye out for a suitable mark when something went wrong and he was found knifed and bleeding to death in a back alley behind a pub. The authorities never brought charges against anyone for his murder. A fact I found deeply unsatisfying as I struggled to understand the loss without a reason behind it.

At the time I blamed our families for his death because, while encouraging his activities, they'd given him no protection, despite their standing in that decidedly dodgy community. We've been estranged ever since.

In a reversal too many, I left Spain and my family, to hide in the small village of Melton. A village I chose by literally sticking a pin in a map. I changed my name from Knight to Fraser and made myself small and unthreatening so as not to attract the attention of anyone from my past. Most would be dead by now, anyway.

When I first met Mr Marchant Senior, I was buried in the depths of my grief at losing George and the life we had planned together. I found myself content to live in this new world of stability and normality. It was only with the arrival of Rex that reminders of my old life returned to me and I began to consider the skills I'd learned and what I could use now to improve my future life.

Although as it turns out I wouldn't have needed to, not if he, aided by his ghastly mother, hadn't stolen what was rightfully mine.

I'd thoroughly enjoyed planning Rex's downfall, and he'd made it so deliciously easy. I carefully laid out all the clues, and researched and put together the paperwork needed to weave into the fabrication of the story I wanted to show.

On the day Rex was due to go on holiday, the day he'd pushed me to my limit, I executed my plan. I did it all and once I found out what he'd cheated me out of, regretted nothing.

And, yes, of course, I was responsible for cancelling his car insurance.

George. Master of the long con. Well, I have just played the longest of my life. And won…

I can hear him now.

'Well done, old girl. I'm proud of you.'

Thank you for taking the time to read *A Stolen Future*. If you enjoyed it, please consider posting a few words as a review on the retail site of your choice, Goodreads and/or BookBub. Or, tell your friends. Word of mouth is an author's best friend and you will feel the warmth of my thanks in the form of a virtual hug. It really does matter as it helps inform other readers whether they should pick up this book or not.

The fifth novel in the *A Shade Darker* series, *Driven by Deceit*, will be released on the 1st May 2026 and will be available to pre-order soon.

1: A Stranger in Town

Stiff muscles complain as I get out of the car, and I arch my back to ease them, rolling my shoulders. The last leg of our journey home was gruelling, and a whimper from the back tells me it was for Scout too. I let her out of her crate, and she bounds over to the grass to relieve herself. We'd had comfort breaks on the way down from Scotland, and perhaps I should have broken the journey with another overnight stay, but once decided on my return, I didn't want any further delay.

It's late, the yard's dark, but I feel the pull of the horses and have to see them before I enter the house. I don't turn on the yard lights, they're too disruptive. Instead, I rely on my phone to cast light into each box. Rooster wanders over to stick his head out of the half-door, and I'm comforted when he blows softly into my palm. I stroke his head, inhaling the familiar scents of horse and hay, which have been absent from my life for long enough.

My holiday had been a much-needed break. The times I'd had to attend court already had been a lot to deal with, and there would be more to come. The divorce proceedings I'd also started had added to my stress.

We'd kept to ourselves at the various places we'd stayed. Scout and I had walked, climbed and scrambled across the Scottish countryside for many miles. Without the distraction of human company for three weeks, I could think about my life and future, which was looking nothing like I'd thought it was going to be only last December.

I complete my circuit of the stables, surprised although pleased to see the last box has a new occupant. This is a welcome sight as it has been empty for too long. I peer over the door at the handsome cob inside and smile. If I'd known whose horse it was, I wouldn't have.

The sound of horses nickering welcomes me to the yard the next morning along with Harry whistling. It's good to hear it again on this beautiful spring morning in early May. My head's groggy as, exhausted by the drive, I overslept, and I lift my face to the sun to absorb some rays. I didn't even hear Harry get up, and he and Pip are already hard at work. As soon as Harry spots me, he runs out of the stable he's in and wraps his arms around me, as enthusiastic as a young Labrador. Pip laughs as she pushes a wheelbarrow past us. 'He's missed you.' And I had him.

'Not that we couldn't cope,' he says, once he's put me down. 'But it's good to see you.' He drags his fingers through his mess of russet-coloured hair and gives me a smile which lights up his face and crinkles the corners of his dark blue eyes.

'It's good to see both of you, too. Can you take a break in five minutes? I'll bring breakfast, but I'd like a debrief.'

Pip's eyes flick to Harry before he answers for them both. 'Sure, we'll just finish off. Tack room?'

I nod then go back to the house to make coffee before returning with a tray for the mugs and, as a small thank you, warm pastries I'd thrown into the oven from my freezer on waking.

Harry O'Connor and Pip Statham, my friends and most trusted workers, had insisted I take the time off, assuring me they could manage everything in my absence. I have complete faith in them but was still reluctant to leave. I'd only agreed to do so when Harry said he'd move into my house to be as close as possible to the horses and they'd both promised to call if anything even approaching an emergency happened in the yard.

The warmth from the sun is far too enticing for us to meet in the windowless tack room, so we drag some crates outside and sit absorbing the heat like lizards after a long winter.

Harry and Pip appear in good spirits, and after a quick rundown, I'm pleased there have been no issues in the yard in my absence and that they've coped excellently. I'm sure they'll appreciate the return of my extra pair of hands to help with getting the work done, though. After my coffee.

'The only thing you haven't mentioned then is the extra horse,' I eventually say, suspicious as to why this was not a leading topic of conversation. They both know how long I've been trying to fill the stable.

'Er, yes.' Harry's eyes immediately slide away from mine as he finishes his third pastry then drains his mug. Pip looks anywhere other than directly at me, fidgets then stands, apparently anxious to get back to mucking out. The mystery deepens.

'What's his name?'

'Houdini.'

'Sounds ominous.'

'Yes, we learned to keep the kick bolt on quickly.'

'Right. Duly noted. How's he settled in?'

'He's grand. Apart from the one escape where he trotted round the yard for a bit saying hello to everyone.' I wince as Harry grimaces. We have a quarantine stable set away from the main block in which to keep a new horse, to stop it touching any others for its first three weeks with us. Just in case. This scenario is therefore hardly ideal, but there was little that could be done once it had happened. Thankfully, it doesn't appear Houdini has brought any diseases into the yard. That would have constituted an emergency and brought me straight home. Harry continues, 'But he was easy to catch and generally he's a chilled character. Eating well. Not fretting or anxious. And he's happy to be with the others now he's in the main yard.' Harry glances at Pip as though for backup and she nods along, although she's chewing her lip, so while Houdini may not be anxious, she is.

'That's good news.' I look from one of them to the other. There's something going on. I can feel it coming at me, but both appear reluctant to talk. 'Whose horse is it?'

'No one you'd know. Cee something or other. I forget the surname. She's moved into Maisie's place.'

'Oh.' I feel a wave of relief as this can only be good news. Not only have we filled a livery space, but Maisie Brooks has a tenant for her cottage, which is directly opposite my house. 'Handy for the yard then.'

'Er, yeah. Although we haven't seen her yet. He's full livery.' I hear an edge of doubt creep into Harry's voice.

'A hands-off owner, eh?' One wonders why some people have horses at all, so infrequently do they visit them. Still, having an extra full livery in the yard will be good for the bank balance, so I can't complain.

'I, er, probably need to tell you something.' My heart sinks. Here it comes.

Get Free Exclusive Content by Signing up to the Georgia Rose Newsletter

You have got this far, so thank you again for reading *A Stolen Future*. I really enjoy interacting with my readers and love to build that relationship via my newsletter. If you sign up to that via my website, I will send you **some content that's only available to my subscribers**, for free.

Acknowledgements

As always, a huge thank you is due to my beta (test) readers. This time Claire Millington, Katherine Winters, Judith Barrow, Kathy Sapsed, Andrew Moore, Debra Cartledge, Clare O'Callaghan and Sarah Postins were exposed to my work at a horribly rough stage as I like early feedback. I thank them for their candour and for telling me what they really thought; it informs my way forward. The excellent feedback has improved this story no end so I thank each and every one of you.

Darlene Foster and Elizabeth Ducie came to my aid at the eleventh hour and I thank them for the extra sets of eyes and wise words.

I was delighted to work with Mark Barry again as he has always been a fierce champion of my books. He took on the task of editor for *A Stolen Future* and in never failing to tell me when my words were not good enough has made it considerably better. Thank you is never enough.

There are countless punctuation and grammar rules and I consider myself truly blessed, and mightily relieved, to have met Julia Gibbs who knows them all! A great big thank you goes to her for her diligence in proofreading my work so that the final product is as polished as it can be. Any errors that remain are mine and mine alone.

I feel fortunate to have been introduced to the wonderfully patient Simon Emery who has designed this fabulous cover and the map. I thank him for his expertise and I am delighted with the end result.

Ideas and inspiration for writing fiction come from many places and I like the facts in my fiction to be as accurate as they can be, so a big thank you goes to an undercover source of mine who provided me with all the police information I needed.

My thanks, as always, goes to the incredibly generous online community of authors, readers, bloggers and reviewers. Much to my surprise, finding all of you has been one of the most enjoyable aspects of becoming an independent author and I thank you for your friendship, knowledge and support.

I thank everyone on my mailing list for signing up to find out more. I love hearing from you and I particularly thank all those who have taken on the challenge of being on my ARC (Advance Reader Copy) team. Your early help (including the error spotting!) and support means a great deal. Let's hope you like what you have just read.

Thank you to all the members of Hunts Writers whose company I enjoy. But a special thank you goes to those of you who organise the group and do all the things I cannot.

Last, but by no means least, is the thank you that goes to my growing family. They have to put up with the actual process of me trying to get a book out and while my grown-up children have now largely escaped most of that, my husband has not. So, Russell, thank you once again for putting up with me through all the times when my thoughts are focused on my fictional world and on getting the work done. x

<u>**Contact details**</u>

Thank you for reading this far. I'm always interested to hear from readers with any feedback, thoughts or observations they are willing to make. If you'd like to get in touch, or you want to hear about what's coming next, I can be found in all of these places:

My website at www.georgiarosebooks.com where you will also have the opportunity to follow my blog or get some free exclusive content by joining my mailing list.

I'm on X/Twitter @GeorgiaRoseBook

On Facebook or you can 'like' the Georgia Rose – Author page.

I'm easy to find on BookBub and Goodreads too, as well as Instagram and Pinterest (although I have absolutely no idea what I'm meant to be doing on those sites!)

Finally, if you have enjoyed reading this, please tell ~~someone~~ *everyone* you know and, whatever you think of it, if you can, would you consider leaving a review? Of whatever rating! You might not think your opinion matters, but I can assure you it does. It helps the book gain visibility, and it informs other readers whether or not to purchase it, so if you could take a minute or two to leave a few words on the retail site of your choice and/or Goodreads and BookBub that would be hugely appreciated.

Now, you're holding a beautiful paperback or hardback in your hand and might be thinking that request doesn't include me... but please think again. It doesn't matter how or where you bought your book, all the sites will still accept a review from you.

Thank you.